**He waits for her in the dark,
knowing she's going to be his...**

Olivia
I've watched him for weeks. I have no idea who he is or why
he holds the key to saving my father's life. But I'm fascinated
by him. And when he catches me breaking into his home, I
shouldn't be so eager to accept the deal he offers: My body
for the answers my dad needs. But when he's finished with
me, will he give me what he promised?

Aiden
I'm fast becoming addicted to the thief I've blackmailed into
my bed. She'll do anything to save her father, the bastard
who's responsible for an unforgivable sin against my family.
Keeping her might require a bigger sacrifice than I'm
willing to make. But losing her would be a crime...

A blistering hot romance with a dominant male and the cat
burglar who steals his heart.

TAKE ME, BREAK ME

TAKE ME, BREAK ME

STEPHANIE JULIAN

MOONLIT NIGHT PUBLISHING

ONE

Olivia

AFTER FIVE ASS-NUMBING hours of surveillance, the light shining through the second-floor window finally dims and I shimmy down the forty-foot oak tree, silent as a shadow.

The only things between me and my prize are the high stone wall topped by an electrified cable and the almost impenetrable system guarding the doors and windows of the massive stone mansion beyond the wall.

Set deep in the hills of northern Berks County, Pennsylvania, the estate sits in the middle of a hundred and fifty acres of dense forest. If you didn't know it's here, you'd never find it. The only way in is a paved lane that rambles through the woods until finally the paving gives way to bare ground and you think you're totally lost.

My dad gave me explicit directions. Now it's up to me

to complete the job. Only this isn't just any other job. This is life and death. My dad's life depends on it. And without my dad, my sister's life will be in danger.

Failure is not an option.

Luckily, Dad taught me well.

Moving through the forest with the surety of two weeks of reconnaissance, I reach my point of entry without incident and start to climb. The rough fieldstone provides plenty of foot- and handholds and I'm at the top of the wall in less than a minute. The live cable at the top would be a problem for someone bigger than me but I'm able to slide beneath without electrocuting myself.

My ear comes within a hair of the cable and electricity whispers against my skin, the fine hair on my neck quivering in anticipation of the shock. A lesser man might've flinched. I'm not a man.

On the other side, I take a second to breathe and center myself before starting my descent. My arm and leg muscles shake but if I drop, I could make too much noise and set off the two dogs. I have tranquilizer darts in my belt, if I need them. I really hope I don't.

Most nights, the man who lives here takes the pure-bred German Shepherds inside with him. They appear to be pets, not guard dogs. The only companions the man has.

During the past two weeks, I've seen no one go inside except a woman who seems to be the housekeeper.

The guy appears to be a hermit. A nameless recluse who never leaves the property owned by a shell company with holdings all over the world. All of my digging never produced a name associated with this company. At least, not a real name.

Someone has gone to an awful lot of trouble to conceal the owner's identity. It's a huge red flag but it's not enough to stop me.

The building had been built more than a century ago by some rich steel magnate as a summer home for his wife and kids. They'd stayed here for about three months out of the year then returned to their New York brownstone or their Pittsburgh mansion. Must've been a nice life.

It'd stayed in the family until about fifty years ago when that owner had been forced to sell the house to cover his alimony. Just another entitled asshole who couldn't keep his dick in his pants. Why did rich people think they'll never get caught?

That's when Squire Incorporated bought it for much less than its value. I have no idea when the man currently occupying the house moved in.

I want to have all the facts I can find when I pull a job like this, especially one as important as this. If I don't have them, I get twitchy. I'm twitchy now. I need the file hidden in the mansion's library. Dad's depending on me. I can't let him or my sister down.

I trip none of the security floodlights as I make my way to the back of the building, where I've identified my entry. A small window on the third floor. The only one not connected to the security system and much too small for a full-grown man to fit through. I'm twenty-five but I'll fit through that window. It'll be tight but not impossible.

The tough part will be the climb. The house is made of

stone but much smoother than the outer wall. Not as many foot- and handholds. And if I fall, I'll fall into the thorny hedges growing around the base of the building. It'll hurt like hell and I'll probably end up with a few holes I don't need or want.

So I can't fall.

Just another day on the job, Livvie.

I hear my dad's voice in my head and shake it out. If I think too much about the situation, I'll get pissed. And when I get pissed, I get irrational. I may even cry. And I can't afford that now.

I've studied the building from every angle and mapped out my climb using photos I've taken, but this is the first time I'm seeing it up close. It's going to be the toughest climb I've ever attempted. With the highest stakes.

Shoving down sudden nerves, I take several deep breaths to center myself once again, forcing down my heart rate. I can do this. I graduated from indoor rock walls to military-grade parkour when I was twelve. Just another climb.

Pulling on my fingerless climbing gloves, I set my grip and start, pulling myself up, inch by inch. I can't go straight to the window. I have to take a zigzag approach, searching for the best holds. I slip about halfway up, feet dangling for a second before I can continue.

My heart races but I take a few moments to still, my toes clad in thin climbing shoes jammed into tiny crevasses in the wall. When I continue, I've managed to shove out every thought but one.

I have to get that file.

It takes me half an hour to reach the window. My muscles sting but I take the time to double-check the window to make sure it's not wired to the alarm system. It's not but it is locked from the inside. I have to open it with one hand. Luckily, it's an old wooden latch. Unluckily, it probably hasn't been opened for years, maybe decades, and it's stuck.

It takes me a good ten minutes to get the damn thing to release, and my arm and leg muscles now scream in protest. I need to get inside, and I need to do it fast.

I swing the window open as slowly as I can, but it still screeches loudly enough to make my breath freeze in my lungs. After a minute of not hearing a sound, I shimmy through the window. It's a tighter fit than I thought it would be, and I'm breathing heavily when I finally land on my feet and take a look around.

Whoa. Not what I'd been expecting.

I thought I'd be in an attic since the window was on the top floor. Dusty floors, cobwebs, lots of junk to maneuver around. Instead, it's a bedroom.

From the moonlight streaming through the window, I can make out the bed on the opposite side of the room. An imposing four-poster with a canopy, which should make it look girly. It doesn't. The dark drapes hanging from the rails look heavy and the bed frame is huge. I wouldn't be surprised if the mattress is bigger than a king.

It looks like a prop in a Victorian horror movie and fits the room perfectly. The walls are papered, the pattern partly shiny and reflecting the moonlight. The rest of the furniture matches the bed. Oversized. Dark wood. Heavily carved.

Ominous.

I shiver for no reason.

The room's empty and I hear nothing from the rest of the house. No alarms, no footsteps pounding up the stairs, no dogs barking. The door to the room is closed and I make my way toward it, only to have my attention drawn to that bed again.

I stop in the middle of the room, my gaze caught on what appear to be ropes holding back the curtains at the head of the bed. They're attached to heavy silver rings on either side of the headboard. There's another ring in the center.

My heart begins to pound and my imagination, not normally overactive, kicks into overdrive. I'm not naïve. I know exactly what you could use those ropes for. My gaze drops to the foot of the bed.

Yep, there are rings on the foot posts and more ropes holding back those curtains. The ropes look almost...delicate. Are there cuffs that attach to those ropes somewhere in the room?

My sex clenches involuntarily, and my next breath rasps in my throat.

Does he tie women to this bed before he fucks them?

Lust rises because I've seen the man who lives here.

No. I can't think about him because if I do...

Another deep breath. I head toward the door. I need to get out of here. Now. I turn the knob and the door opens without a sound. I'd been expecting a creak at least. But no, this door swings on well-oiled hinges. Someone uses this room regularly.

I swallow hard, images crowding my brain of what the man might do in this room. What I'd allow him to do to me in this room.

Focus.

Sliding into the hallway, I make my way to the stairs in front of me. There's another doorway to the left but I'm not here to explore. I know exactly where I'm going.

I stop at the top of the stairs and listen. Hearing nothing, I start my descent.

The wide stairs don't creak either. This place is a thief's paradise.

I don't linger on the second floor, merely stop to make sure the coast is clear before continuing down a grand curved staircase, my fingers trailing along the cool wood of the banister. I've never seen anything as beautiful as the carving on the handrail. And I've been in some expensive homes before.

Finally, I reach the first floor. The stairs drop me into a huge foyer, complete with marble tiled floors and arched front door. Totally castle chic.

Who the hell lives like this? Certainly not me or anyone I know. This is a whole other level beyond what I'm used to.

Some slight sound from the left catches my ear and I freeze. It repeats and I realize it's the sound of an icemaker.

Can it really be this easy?

I'm beginning to wonder at my luck. I still haven't seen the two dogs I know live here. I did see them earlier tonight. The man had let them out to run just before eleven.

Maybe they sleep with their master. More likely, they're somewhere on the first floor.

But as I make my way to the back of the house and the library I know is there, I don't hear them. No whining, no nails on the wood floors, no barking.

Something nudges at the back of my brain, something telling me to get the hell out of here.

But I can't. Not without the file.

I set off through the front hall, which might be as big as my entire apartment, and through the entrance to the room behind the stairs.

The library is almost pitch black because the windows are covered. I know the general layout but I need light because I don't want to accidentally bump into anything. I grab the tiny flashlight from my belt and flick it on.

During the day, the curtains in this room are open and I'd been able to get some decent shots of the interior. I know where the desk and the safe are located.

I should head there immediately but I take a second to swing the light around the room.

It really is straight out of a fairytale.

I may be a thief but I was once a little girl who wanted to be Belle. A little girl who loved to read and play with dolls and pretend that someday, she'd grow up and marry a prince.

That was before I'd realized life doesn't have fairytale endings. But it does have absent mothers and sick sisters and fathers who worked well outside the law.

And now I'm starring in my own private version of a gender-swapped Aladdin. Progressive, right?

Still, sometimes I wonder what it'd be like to be the princess instead of the thief. And to have a prince present me with a library like this.

God, this place is so far removed from my reality that I'm still not sure it isn't the set for a movie.

The room is circular, the walls curved, and books cover every inch of those walls. Above, there's a painted ceiling that looks like stained glass. I'm not sure if it's a pattern or a picture and I don't have the time to find out now.

If this were a movie, I'd be about to get my ass caught right about now. So I drag my attention away from all the lovely books and that ceiling and focus instead on the massive wooden desk in front of the window across the room.

The flashlight reveals intricate carving on the front but I've already spent way too much time here. I need to get what I came for and get the hell out.

I hurry to the other side of the desk and check the drawers. They're all open, no locks. I guess when you live alone and with this much security, you don't worry about anyone stealing your shit.

The only other person I'd seen in the house besides him is the housekeeper who works four days a week.

Like I said, the man's a hermit. In the two weeks I've watched the house, I've only ever seen him leave once. I have no idea where he went in his fancy Lexus that probably cost more than I'd make at a legitimate job in two years.

I guess I'm lucky I don't have to rely on that legitimate job to live. I've been building my reputation since I was sixteen. I hope to be able to retire before I'm forty. Or before I get caught. Like my dad.

I don't blame him for getting caught. It can happen to the best. But what he's been threatened with makes me want to puke. And to stab someone.

But I'll clean up his mess because of Maylyn. She doesn't deserve what she's been threatened with. Jesus, she's only twenty.

A search of the desk reveals nothing so I'm left with the safe. I've already been here an hour. I need to be gone by five thirty a.m. when the guy wakes. I have about two hours. And it's going to take me at least fifteen minutes to crack the safe.

I turn toward the wall that divides the library from the rest of the house and head for the large still life hanging on it. Swinging it out reveals the door of the safe. State of the art...five years ago.

I've cracked a hundred of these. Still, my palms get sweaty inside my gloves and my heart rate increases. Some of it's performance anxiety. Most of it's the thrill of the challenge.

I retrieve the stethoscope from my belt and get to work. The dial spins beneath my fingers and my breathing immediately levels out.

I'm in the zone.

Ten minutes later, I turn the handle and the door opens. Now I hold my breath. If the file isn't here...

I shine the flashlight into the darkness of the safe and suck in a breath.

Jewelry boxes. A pile of cash. And files.

It seems too good to be true. I've learned that most things usually are.

Doesn't matter. I need the file.

I pull them all out one at a time. Of course, it's the very last file, placed against the far wall, almost out of reach.

I leaf through the pages, just to make sure everything I need is there, then I stuff it into the back of my pants and pull my shirt over it, make sure it's secure then close the safe and swing the painting back over it.

It's three twenty-five a.m. More than enough time to get out of here before he wakes.

I take my time up the stairs. Don't want to rush now. I'm almost home free.

I reach the bedroom. Slide through the door and close it behind me.

I open the window.

"Did you find what you need?"

TWO

Aiden

I HAD a feeling she'd come tonight.

Anticipation runs through my body like an electric charge, making my heart pound and my breathing quicken.

I tell myself it's because I can finally finish what I started, but some part of my brain knows that's not true.

I ignore that and concentrate on not making a sound as I head from my hiding place on the third floor to the attic bedroom while she enters the library below.

It's been almost two weeks since she started watching the house. I knew she'd make her move soon. The countdown to save her father is getting closer to zero and Olivia will do everything she can to save him.

What she doesn't know is that she needs to save him from me.

And she's about to learn just how much it's going to cost her.

Watching her through the security system feed on my phone, I know she's found the safe and is making her way back up the staircase.

Damn, the girl moves like a gymnast. No, like a trained dancer. I'd gotten hard watching her climb the wall of the house like she's fucking Spider-Man.

Hell, if I'm honest, I'll admit I get hard anytime I see Olivia. I tell myself it's because she's beautiful and any man who sees her wants her. But I know that's bullshit.

There's something about this woman that makes me want to fuck her.

And I'm going to. She's going to give me what I want tonight and I'm going to take back what she needs to save her father. Then I'm going to watch the bastard twist in the wind before I shut him down.

I can't fucking wait. The smile on my face would probably terrify her. Tough shit.

She's a thief. A good one, by all accounts. But she's still a thief. Tonight, she'll learn what it's like to be on the opposite side. Tonight, I'm going to steal what she needs so desperately.

Then I'm going to send her back to her father and watch the trap close around him.

Through the security feed, I see she's reached the second floor. Where she pauses, looking at the closed doors. At my bedroom door, in particular.

Of course she knows which one it is. She's been watching the house for two weeks. I made no effort to hide the fact that that's the room I sleep in. But why is she staring at it?

I want to see her expression but the darkness and the grainy quality of the feed skews my vision.

There's no way in hell she's looking at my door with anything other than fear. Maybe she thinks she heard something. Maybe she's being overly cautious. Maybe...

In the next second, she shakes her head and continues to the stairs to the third floor.

To me.

Now my heart thumps against my ribs like a trapped animal, and again I tell myself it's simply the fact that I'm going to finish what Granddad couldn't. It doesn't have anything to do with feelings. I have no feelings for this girl.

She's a means to an end. The fact that I want her is irrelevant. It just means—

A pang of something I refuse to call guilt hits me. I'm not going to take anything she won't freely give. I'm just not going to let her have her prize at the end of the night.

She'll hate me but who cares? I certainly won't.

She's almost to the top of the staircase now and I sit a little straighter in the chair facing the door, in the darkest corner of the room. She might not see me before I make my presence known. Then again, she might realize I'm there and try to run. She won't get far. All of the other windows and doors are locked down tight and there's nowhere for her to run unless she breaks a window.

I don't think she'll run.

I think she's smart enough to know it won't help her situation.

When she puts her hand on the doorknob, I put my phone down, that sense of anticipation rising until my lungs hurt.

I force myself to relax as the door opens and she steps into the room.

Finally.

Her form is a dark shadow as she closes the door silently behind her. I'm in the room with her and I don't hear her make a sound as she runs to the window.

I let her put hand on the window and swing it open before I say, "Did you find what you need?"

She freezes, so still I swear she's not breathing.

Then she moves as if to jump through the window.

"I wouldn't do that if I were you. The dogs will be on you in seconds. Why don't you turn around?"

She doesn't comply right away. I didn't expect her to. Frankly, I expect her to jump. To try to, at least. I wouldn't have let her. She'd hurt herself and that's not how I want this night to end.

"Olivia, please. I'm not going to hurt you. Have a seat. I want to talk."

She flinches when I say her name but stays with her back to me.

I don't want to have to get physical. Yet. But I will if she leaves me no choice.

A second later, she straightens away from the wall and turns. There's enough light streaming in from the window that I can see her clearly now.

My cock hardens even more.

I know from the investigator's report that her mother

was part Japanese and part Italian. And her father is some combination of English, German, and French.

And she's a fucking beautifully exotic combination of genes with straight black hair, pale gray eyes, sharp cheekbones, and a mouth so perfect I want to devour her.

At least for this one night.

When the sun comes up, she leaves and I go on with my life.

Her gaze meets mine and I see defiance in the line of her mouth. She looks like a teenager but she's twenty-five. More than old enough to understand exactly how much trouble she's in. How much danger.

Though she doesn't know it, I won't physically hurt her. That goes beyond the line I've drawn. But she will give me what I want.

"You know my name."

Her voice holds only a hint of roughness. No accent. It makes the small hairs on my body stand on end.

"I know a lot more than that."

Her head tilts to the side, the single braid containing her long hair falling over her shoulder as her eyes narrow. I want to wrap that braid around my fist and draw her closer.

"Then I'm at a disadvantage."

"Yes, you are."

I don't say anything else, just watch her. She shows no sign of worry or distress, simply holds my gaze.

I want to smile because I like that about her. Unafraid to back down. Good.

Settling deeper into the chair, like I had all the time in

the world, I hold her attention. I can practically see the gears in her head working, trying to find a way out of here.

When her jaw clenches almost imperceptibly, I know she realizes there is none.

"What do you want?" She finally asks the million-dollar question.

I don't hide my smile. "We'll start with the file you stole."

Her expression doesn't change. "I don't know what you're talking about."

"Of course you do."

Her pointed chin lifts. "If you think I've stolen something, aren't you going to call the police?"

"No need for them to be involved. Not if you cooperate."

Her gaze narrows for a second. "And if I don't?"

I shrug. "Why wouldn't you? You've been caught. You're not leaving until you hand over the file."

"Why do you think I've stolen anything?"

"Because I've been watching your every move since you jumped the wall. I have to say, I've never seen anything like your climb up the building. Amazing."

Her expression doesn't change. "Thank you. Why aren't you going to call the police?"

"They'd just get in the way."

I hear her breath hitch and I wonder if I've frightened her. I didn't think it'd be that easy. And I don't want her to be frightened. I know that sounds ridiculous but I don't want to scare her.

I want her to fight. I want her to be brave. Call me twisted, but I don't want her to come to me frightened.

I want her to approach the deal I'm about to offer as I would. A means to an end.

"Don't be frightened, Olivia."

"Shouldn't I be?" There goes that chin again. "I'm an intruder in your home. If you're not going to call the cops, why shouldn't I assume you're going to do something much worse to me?"

"I told you. I'm not going to harm you."

"And I'm supposed to take your word for it?"

I rise to my feet and watch as she locks her knees, refusing to retreat. I force back a smile.

"What possible reason could I have to lie?"

She holds my gaze steadily. "What reason does anyone have to lie? What do you want?"

I walk to the door and open it wider. "Have a drink with me."

Her gaze narrows again and I can tell she's trying to figure out my angle. She's also trying to figure out if she can make it out the window before I could catch her.

She must realize she can't because she sucks in a deep breath and walks toward me. She moves like a dancer and I can't help but admire the sway of her hips. When she's within touching distance, she stops, as if to show me she's not afraid. But I see the wariness in her eyes and in the stiffness of her shoulders.

I wave her through the door. "I think you know where the library is."

She flinches slightly as she walks by me into the hall

then heads for the staircase. This allows me to watch her ass. The woman is all sleek muscle and contained energy. I want to run my hands down her arms and back up her ribs, pet the flawless skin almost completely covered by her black clothing.

Her skintight black pants cling to every curve of her ass and her shirt lovingly outlines breasts that are barely more than a handful. Still, I want to put my mouth on them and see if I can make her come just by sucking on her nipples.

Christ. My balls ache already and I haven't touched her. Couldn't touch her. Not yet. Not until she says yes.

And she will say yes.

I follow a few feet behind, not close enough to crowd her but not far enough away for her to forget that I'm there.

Not that I think she'll forget me. I'm pretty sure I'm the number one thought in her head right now. The second is trying to figure out how to get away from me.

I say nothing as we walk back down the two flights of stairs. I catch glimpses of her face as we reach the second floor and then again on the curved stairs to the first floor.

Her expression remains blank but I see her gaze dart to the front door. She can't outrun me. I'd have my hand on her arm in a few seconds flat.

But it doesn't mean she doesn't think about running. I like that about her. I love watching her brain work. Even if I can't read her mind, I know she's thinking about ways to get away.

At the bottom of the stairs, she stops and turns to stare at me. "I'd prefer to remain here for our little talk."

In the open, with access to all the windows and doors.

She has to know those doors are locked and the windows are bulletproof. She'd only hurt herself if she tried to break through them.

"And I prefer to be comfortable."

I wave a hand toward the library in the back of the house and, after a short, indrawn breath, she begins to move again. Now, I see nerves encroaching. Her steps are shorter and her head jerks left then right, as if planning her exit route.

I half expect her to take off for the kitchen and attempt to lose me long enough to somehow get out of the house. Maybe she knows about the stairway from the kitchen to the upper levels, the one that used to be for the staff.

I don't have a house staff except for Margaret, the housekeeper who's been with my family for more than thirty years. She's the only person I trust to have the access codes to any of my personal properties.

Without her, I would've had to learn to cook. I give a silent chuckle at the thought. Margaret would be laughing her ass off if I even suggested it.

Margaret would be pissed as hell if she knew what I was up to tonight. Then again, she's known me all my life. She knows all my faults. And she still works for me.

Sometimes, that amazes me. Then I remember how much I'm paying her and realize my dad was right when he said everyone has their price. Some people's price is higher than anyone is willing to pay. Some can be had for the right amount of money.

I'm about to find out how much Olivia is willing to pay for her father's sins.

We reach the library seconds later and I can tell she's about to bolt. Probably for one of the dark corners on the far side of the room.

Flipping the switches at the side of the door, I flood the room with light and watch her blink to adjust her eyes.

Shutting the door behind me, I lock it with the key and shove it in the pocket of my jeans.

Her gaze follows my every move. And now I see fear in her eyes.

Can't be helped. She can't be allowed to run. Not with the file. And not until I've had her.

I've been fantasizing about spreading her out on top of that monstrosity of a desk and fucking her until she screams my name since this plan first took shape.

"I've got whiskey, vodka, bourbon, rum. Preference?"

"To be allowed to leave."

I smile and her eyes widen. Not sure if I've frightened her even more or simply surprised her. Whichever it is, she's warier now. Her body stiffens and her expression sets in a way that makes me want to know exactly what she's thinking.

And even though I know she won't tell me, I'm still going to ask.

"What's going through your head right now?"

The chin goes up again. "You can keep me here against my will but you can't make me tell you what I'm thinking."

I shrug and turn back to the small bar. I pour two glasses of whiskey, set one on the low table, and sink into one of the matching overstuffed chairs that flank it.

This room is the one room in the house, besides my bedroom, that I took a personal interest in decorating.

It's my favorite room of this house, the one my father had bought years ago for my mother. But she'd been gone before he had the chance to bring her here. Or maybe she ran because she knew if he'd gotten her here, she'd never have left.

I have no illusions about my father, but I have a shitton of resentment where my mother is concerned. Some call it an obsession. They're probably right.

It takes her a full thirty seconds to consider her options before she swallows hard and slides into the chair opposite me.

Leaning back into the cushions, I watch her lift the glass then take a delicate sniff followed by a healthy swallow.

Can't blame her for needing the liquid courage. Maybe it'll loosen her up a little, though I'm not holding out for a miracle.

"So," I start. "The file."

She seems to have gotten a better handle on her emotions because she stares straight into my eyes and says, "Go to hell."

I smile. "I've been. Why do you need the file?"

Her gaze narrows as if she's learned something to use against me. "If you know so much about me, you know the answer to that question."

"Let's say, for the sake of argument, that I don't. Enlighten me."

"And if I do, will you let me leave with it?"

That will never happen but I'm willing to play along to get what I want.

"Convince me I should."

She takes a few breaths before taking another sip of whiskey. Her gaze drops to the glass I hold in my hand. Is she wondering if she can outdrink me?

I'm six-two and weigh two hundred pounds. I'm by no means a muscle-bound gorilla but I don't miss too many workouts. I can run a 5K in twenty minutes and swim twenty laps without stopping. I take care of my body because you never know when it might turn on you.

She'll never be able to drink me under the table.

Finally, she leans back into the chair, mimicking my casual stance. But she's just as ready as I am.

"What if I told you it's a matter of life and death?"

My eyebrows rise. "Yours?"

For the briefest second, she sucks her bottom lip between her teeth and bites down before releasing it.

Why the fuck do I find that so amazingly erotic? It makes me want her to use those teeth on me. All over. It also means I want to use my teeth on her and my mouth waters just thinking about where I'd use them first.

My gaze falls to her throat then lower, to her breasts. Are her nipples tight and pointed or am I seeing things that aren't there?

Can she really be as turned on as I am right now?

Because if she is, this whole revenge-fuck scenario could blow up in my face.

THREE

Olivia

TWO WEEKS of watching him have made me crazy.

That's the only explanation I have for the way I feel about the man staring like he wants to take a bite of me.

Yes, he's handsome but I knew that. There's something about him that makes my breath catch. Not many men have done that. The few who have, I slept with.

Probably not a good comparison right now.

He's not conventionally handsome. His features are a little too broad, his eyes a little too intense. And that hair. It falls past his shoulders and looks like he hasn't combed it for days, just ran his hands through it to keep it out of his eyes.

He'd look like some crazed hermit if not for the fact that the body under those jeans and long-sleeved t-shirt is honed to my idea of perfection.

All right, maybe I might have developed a little crush on the mark. But no other woman I know would blame me if they'd seen him the way I have.

Especially if they'd seen him naked and just out of the shower.

Like I have.

I still have no idea who he is and curiosity is eating me alive, even though he's caught me stealing and now has me locked in a room with him in a mansion straight out of a horror movie miles from the nearest house.

And no one knows I'm here. Not my dad, not Maylyn. Not Bryant or Reese.

Damn it, what had I done wrong?

The answer is nothing. My surveillance isn't at fault. No, someone had to have tipped him off. The question is... What do I do now?

He's made no attempt to hurt me but I know he can. He can probably snap my arm with one hand. Knock me out with a single blow to the head.

The fact that he hasn't makes him that much more dangerous.

And when he stares at me like he is now, with that level of intensity, I want to climb on his lap and stick my tongue down his throat.

Yeah, that's definitely crazy. And possibly creepy.

Although now that we're in the same room together and he holds my fate in his hands...

Maybe I'm in shock. I've never been caught before. Sure, I've had a couple of close calls but no one has ever seen my face.

Shock is the only reason I can come up with for how I feel about this man.

So what now?

I haven't responded to his last question and, from the look on his face, he's still waiting for an answer.

He'd asked if my life was in danger. I could lie but I have a feeling he'd know. I'm pretty sure he already knows why I need the file.

Which leads me back to the idea that I've been set up.

I need answers and the only way to get them is to give some. I just need to be smart about it.

"No, not my life. Someone close to me."

"Someone you love."

"Yes."

His expression doesn't change. "And why should I care?"

Does he want me to beg him to save my family's life? There's no reason at all for him to care. How do I appeal to him?

"Because you're not a monster."

His eyebrows rise slightly though I can only see one. The other disappears under the fall of hair across that side of his face. "How do you know that? What do you think you know about me?"

He sits back in his chair like he doesn't have a care in the world. And why would he? I'm the one he caught breaking into his home. He could call the cops at any time and I'd be taken away. Hell, he could do anything at all to me and no one would know. We're completely alone.

But I won't go down without a fight.

"Actually, I don't know your name." If I'm going to get through this, I can't show any fear. "I have no idea who you are or why you choose to live in the middle of nowhere, alone except for two dogs, with no visitors except a housekeeper."

His mouth quirks into a slight smile. "You've been thorough."

Probably best to keep my mouth shut about that.

"I'm desperate."

Shit. That came out a little more raw than I'd intended.

My breath hitches in my chest. The stakes are too high for me to fail. I have to find some way to leave the house with that file.

"So you'd be willing to do anything for that file."

He didn't phrase it as a question. He knew he had me by the short hairs.

I answer anyway. "Yes."

He stares at me for several more seconds and I try to control my breathing. Conflicting emotions of fear and lust wreak havoc on my body. I'm hot and cold, shaky and still, all at the same time.

I'd said yes and I mean it. I'll do anything for this file.

"So if I tell you to strip and lie across that desk, you'll do it?"

Shock makes me freeze. Then heat flushes through my body on a rush of adrenaline.

My cheeks burn and I'm pretty sure they're bright red. My lungs ache with the need for oxygen but I don't want to gasp.

I do not want to be aroused by him.

Can I really be attracted to a man who could force me to do anything he wants? Will he force me to have sex with him? Or does he want to humiliate me?

And will I really be that upset if he does want to have sex with me?

Watching his every move has obviously made me insane.

"I guess I need to know if you plan to hurt me."

His mouth loses the slight grin. "I'm not a sadist."

"Then what are you?"

Those dark eyebrows rise again. "I'm a man whose private property you have stuffed in your pants."

I hadn't forgotten it was there but now I feel the paper file sticking to the sweaty skin of my back.

He shifts slightly in his chair and I watch his every move with growing fascination.

Now that I'm in the same room with him, I sense a wildness about him, which is probably just fantasy on my part.

Maybe I'm trying to talk myself into actually doing what he wants. However, I'm usually a better negotiator than this.

"So I show you my naked body and you let me leave with the file. Is that the deal?"

He shrugs. "I never said that was all I wanted."

My jaw sets. "Then what do you want?"

I can't keep the frustration out of my voice now. My brain has been running at high speed, trying to keep up with him. I'm pretty damn smart but I have a feeling I've met my mental match.

I don't think I'm going to be able to talk my way out of this situation. And if I'm honest, I'm not sure I want to.

There's a part of me that wants him, that wants to give him exactly what he asked for. Although he didn't actually ask for it.

"Maybe I want more than just to look at your naked body. Maybe I want to touch you."

My heart pounds against my ribs and my mouth waters thinking about him putting his hands on me.

I can't help it. My gaze drops to his knees, where his hands rest. They're huge. And scarred. And I don't mean like average, everyday scars from nicks and scratches. I mean, they're both covered with large, ropy scars over the back and probably the palms.

I can't help but wonder what happened to them.

When my gaze finally returns to his, the intensity in those eyes has deepened. As has the color. His brown eyes now look almost black.

I hadn't been able to tell from my surveillance but this close, they were mesmerizing.

But I'm not here on a date. I can't afford to be sidetracked.

"And if I agree?"

I should be horrified. And seriously terrified that this man holds my fate in his hands.

Instead, I sit here fantasizing about him putting those hands on me.

I've been told before that I'm damaged, that I have no

morals, which is completely untrue. I have a strong moral code. I never steal from anyone who would suffer from the loss. Because I'm good and can command high prices for my services, I have the ability to turn down any job I don't want. Much of what I steal has been obtained illegally and can be returned to its rightful owner.

Yes, I know I'm breaking the law but I also know that my methods are more...humane than others.

I've never had a job that involved bloodshed. I've also never been caught before. I've also never taken as much of an interest in a mark as I have with this one.

Maybe my brain is a little more warped than I thought because I'm getting excited.

His head tilts to the side, as if he's considering his answer, but his gaze never leaves mine.

Finally, he leans forward in his chair and I instinctively lean back. His eyes narrow, the only sign that he notices my reaction. Lifting his glass from the table, he takes a swallow and now I watch his throat.

Oh my god, I've got to stop. This is ridiculous.

"I agree not to harm you in any way."

His voice sends a shiver down my spine. I can't believe I'm contemplating his offer.

Actually, that's not right. I know exactly why I'm contemplating his offer and it has as much to do with the ache in the pit of my stomach as it does with the life-and-death nature of why I need the file.

"And you'll allow me to leave tomorrow morning. With the file. Without calling the police."

His expression shows no sign of triumph or gloating.

"You'll be able to walk out the front door. No strings attached, no cops. The information is yours to do with as you want."

It's too easy. There has to be strings attached.

And still, I know I'm going to take the deal because it's the best I can hope for.

"Then I accept."

FOUR

Aiden

I HEAR HER WORDS AND, even though I knew she'd agree, I'm shocked she accepts so quickly.

Lust roars through my body on a wave that threatens to drown out rational thought. That's dangerous. Even though it's only lust, I have to keep it under control. I'll take her tonight and send her on her way when the sun comes up. And I'll get part of the satisfaction I crave.

Her father deserves every ounce of pain coming his way. She's merely the vessel to provide it.

The fact that she's a beautiful vessel means nothing except that fucking her won't be painful. Far from it.

Now that she's agreed, I don't want to waste any time. I'm going to renege on one of the promises she believes I've made in good faith but not all. She'll walk out of here unharmed when the sun rises.

I rise to my feet, towering over her, but she doesn't cringe. She has to tilt her head back to maintain eye contact, baring her throat, and I have the overwhelming urge to wrap my hand around her neck and pull her against me so I can devour her mouth.

Instead, I turn, walk to the chair behind the desk, and sink into it. It's not a traditional desk chair, it's a wing chair, and I slouch back into it, waiting for the show to begin.

With baited breath. My cock is already hard, although I hope like hell she can't tell.

It takes her several long seconds to respond. She blinks, the only outward sign of nervousness and, finally, she moves. She rises from the chair with a sinuous grace that makes it hard for me to stay still. I want to reach for her and pull her onto my lap.

My body likes that idea and my fingers dig into the arms of the chair for several seconds before I consciously relax them.

She walks to the desk, the formfitting black top and pants she's wearing highlighting every slight curve.

Stopping on the other side of the desk, she puts her hands on her hips and looks me straight in the eyes.

I see a challenge there and I want to grin but I bite it back. I've told her the terms. I'm allowing her the choice of how she wants to do this.

I don't really expect a striptease. I figure she'll shed her clothes as fast as possible, throw them in my face in defiance then stand there and stare me down, unafraid and unashamed.

Instead, she holds my gaze and lifts her top up and over her head as if she were undressing for a lover.

It's a good tactic. It might have set another man back.

It settles me, allows me to breathe and enjoy the show.

And it is a show.

She's attempting to take the upper hand. It's not going to happen but I'll let her have the moment.

Of course, she's nowhere close to being naked. Beneath the shirt, she's wearing a black sports bra that covers everything important. No cleavage, not at all sexy.

Except it is, because now I can't wait to see what's beneath.

But she's not ready to allow that. She reaches for the snap on her pants and pops it with an audible click. My gaze drops at the sound and I see the quiver of her belly. I plan to lick my way up that stomach to her breasts and down again to her pussy, where I'm going to make her come with my tongue.

The thought makes my mouth water and I grind my back teeth. Her gaze drops to my jaw and I see her lips twitch at the corners. She doesn't actually smile but I can tell she wants to.

I'm going to wipe that expression away soon enough.

Reaching behind her to remove the file from her pants, she puts it on the desk in front of her.

I don't even look at it.

Now, her hands go to the zipper to release it before she shoves the pants down her thighs.

Before I can get a good look at her, she bends at the waist, dragging the pants with her. I see the line of her spine and she looks so damn slight, my hand might actually span her entire back.

When she straightens, I see the first sign of nerves.

She blinks several times and her gaze drops to the floor for long seconds before she meets mine again.

Part of me wants to pity her. And part of me knows she's nothing more than the means to an end. And I didn't lie. I will never physically hurt her.

I see her fingers shake slightly as she reaches for the band of her bra and pulls it over her head. It's stretchy but tight and doesn't give as easily as her shirt. She has to twist her torso to get it over her breasts, and her body moves in a way that makes my mouth dry.

I knew it would be no chore to fuck her. But maybe I hadn't counted on how much I want to put her under me.

I can't let that send me off track. I have a plan. Which doesn't mean I can't enjoy her. Hell, I definitely plan to enjoy her.

And the aftermath...even more.

Finally, she works the bra over her head and stands in front of me almost naked. Her breasts are a little bigger released from their confinement and I find it increasingly hard to breathe.

I should cut myself some slack. I tell myself I'm just as turned on by her nudity as I am by knowing I'll finally have my revenge on her father.

I let my gaze travel from her breasts down to her panties then up again to her face.

She knows what I want. I only have to lift my eyebrows to make her swallow hard then move her hands to her panties. Her chin lifts slightly as she works her thumbs into the waistband then pushes down. Her hips shift and my fingers curl into the arms of the chair.

Air is scarce once again and I breathe in through my nose though I don't let my gaze drop immediately.

Her cheeks are pinker now and I find it harder to control my reaction.

She's obviously aroused and that feeds my desire. My cock throbs against my zipper and I want to release the pressure, but I know my limits. If I unzip my pants now, she'll be under me in seconds.

And I don't want this to be over so quickly. I want her to enjoy it. I want her to want it as much as I do.

Then I want to send her back to her father without the file he needs to save his life.

I've been living for this moment for years and I'm sure that's part of the reason I'm so aroused.

Yes, she's pretty and I want to fuck her but she's not my normal type. Lately I haven't had a normal type. Just women I pay to have sex with me. Blonde, brunette, redhead. Dark skin, fair skin. I haven't cared. As long as they agree to the terms.

And they all do. They get paid enough.

This one's not getting paid, though, is she? No, she's the one who's going to pay.

"Now what?"

Her voice doesn't shake but there's something in her tone that makes me want to grin. She's just as turned on as I am.

Good. That's good. I want her with me every step of the way.

"Come around to this side."

I push my chair farther way from the desk, the tiny rollers under the legs allowing it to move easily, giving her more than enough space to stand between me and the desk.

She hesitates now, her lips tightening as if she wants to say something but can't find the right words. The only word I'll accept is yes.

She must know this because after several seconds, she finally moves.

Her motions aren't as smooth as they were before. She's hesitant and I wonder if she's considering reneging. Or running. I wouldn't put it past her.

But she has nowhere to go and everything to lose if she does.

Of course, she's going to lose everything anyway.

Finally, she's standing in front of me, and if I wasn't so set on my mission, I might actually be a little in awe of her.

She's all sleek muscle and gentle curves, and my jaw sets. The dark hair at the juncture of her thighs is trimmed short and I'm pretty sure she shaves between her legs. I want her to sit on the edge of the desk so I can put my mouth over her and use my tongue to fuck her.

I want her to grab my hair and pull until it hurts. I've let it grow because getting it cut hasn't been a priority. I'm not the face of the company. I prefer to work behind the scenes, out of the spotlight. When I get sick of it, I'll have it cut off, though I admit I've gotten used to the length.

As if she's read my mind, her gaze falls to my shoulders, where my hair hangs over by at least two inches. She probably thinks I look homeless but I'm not here to impress her.

I'm here to make her father pay for his crimes.

But first, unless she fights me, which I don't think she will, I'll make her scream when she comes.

"Sit on the edge of the desk."

My voice has a definite growl now. I need to get that under control.

Finally, she balks. Her hands clench into fists for several seconds before she releases them. "No. Whatever you want, you can do it while I'm standing."

My mouth curves into a smile, which contributes, I'm sure, to her hesitancy.

"I can think of a few things I want to do to you while you're standing but right now I want you on the desk."

She swallows hard. "And if I refuse?"

I shrug. "Then you leave without your precious file."

I see her weigh the options and I wonder if maybe she does have a breaking point. If there's a limit to what she'll do for her father. The bastard doesn't deserve her devotion. Not after what he's done.

Then she takes a step back, puts her hands on the desk behind her, and lifts herself onto the top. The wood must be cool beneath her ass and thighs because a shiver works through her body.

She manages to get herself situated without spreading her legs and now I'm aching for a glimpse of her pussy. My jaw shifts and I resist the urge to tell her to spread her legs.

I will soon enough. And then I'll put my mouth on her. For now, I just stare. But something bothers me.

"Release your hair."

The words are out before I realize I'm going to speak. Now her jaw sets, resolute.

"No."

I let my smile grow. "Then I guess I'll just have to do it myself. That's okay. I was getting up anyway."

I rise to my feet, her gaze glued to mine, and close the few steps between us. I stop centimeters from her knees, so close I swear I can feel the heat of her body through my jeans.

I stare down at her for several long seconds, her dark eyes widening, whether in surprise or fear, I'm not sure. Since I don't want her to fear me, at least not now, I try to soften my stance.

But it's not happening because nothing about me is soft now. Every muscle in my body is tense, my cock hard as stone, and my mind focused on only one thing. Making her comply.

I lift my arm and she doesn't flinch but her eyes widen as she watches me reach for the braid at the nape of her neck.

My fingers brush against the skin of her shoulders and she swallows so hard I can hear her. I grip the braid in my hand and bring it around to the front. I flick off the rubber band at the end and let the silky strands spill through my fingers.

Her hair is stick-straight and so black it has blue highlights. It falls over her shoulder and covers one breast. It's sexy as fuck but I want to see her breasts so I push it aside, letting my fingers brush her nipple. The tip is tight and puckered and it's all I can do to hold myself back from putting my mouth over it and sucking hard.

She can't control her breathing any longer and her chest rises and falls at an ever-increasing pace. I'm having the same problem but I refuse to rush. I've been planning this night for months, planning this revenge, and she's not going to entice me into rushing.

Whether she leaves at daybreak or sunset tomorrow doesn't matter. I'll have had her and that's all that matters.

But first, I have to know.

With my hands centimeters from her breast, I lift my head and stare into her eyes. Hers have widened even more and her lips are trembling and slightly parted.

Holy fuck. She's sex incarnate.

Sucking in air as discreetly as I can, I say, "Are you sure you don't want to leave? Without the file, of course...but with your clothes."

She takes several seconds to answer and I force myself not to hold my breath, to breathe as naturally as I can.

"I'm not leaving without the file."

Her voice isn't as strong as it was earlier but the resolution is still there. The breathy quality of her voice makes my balls tighten and my cock throbs against my zipper so hard, it's going to bear the imprint.

Triumph floods me with heat and I let the lust have free rein.

FIVE

Olivia

THE LUST in his eyes lights an answering fire deep in my gut.

I've never had a reaction to any other man like I'm having to this one. A man holding me against my will— But that's not true, is it?

I agreed to stay and allow him to do whatever he wants to me so I can leave with that file. He says he won't hurt me and, for some insane reason, I believe him.

Something about the way he stares at my hair as it hangs over my shoulder. I can't explain it. I just know he won't hit me. Yes, he may bite but it would be with my consent. And that's shocking because I've never been the kind of person who wanted that.

With this man, I feel like I'm allowed to let loose. I

mean, I'm at his mercy and I've put myself there deliberately.

It's almost as if I'm in control. Which is foolish. I know that. I still—

He leans forward, brushing my hair away from my breast, and puts his lips over my nipple.

Shock runs through me like an electric charge. I grab the edge of the desk to hold myself steady, I'm already so close to the edge of orgasm.

Between the adrenaline rush and the fear and the carnality of the situation, I'm surprised I haven't dissolved into a pile of shaking bones.

But I am my father's daughter. Trained by the best. Untouchable.

Until now.

And even though he's only touching me with his lips, he's drowning my ability to think clearly under a flood of sensation.

His lips are soft but the suction on my breast is strong. My back arches involuntarily, trying to make him take more of me, or suck harder, or do something. I don't really know what I want him to do.

He has his own agenda, however.

His lips work my nipple as if he's been starved and can't get enough. The desk is high enough that he doesn't have to bend much but I can tell it's still a strain. If I lie back, he'd have an easier time. And much more access.

But I know that's not what I should be thinking. I should be divorcing myself from the situation. Not enjoying it.

And yet...

After the past two weeks, I have to admit I'm fascinated by him. Maybe a little obsessed.

Maybe a lot obsessed.

Yes, he holds my fate in his hands but those hands are huge and I've dreamed about him putting them on me. Dreamed about him using them to stroke me and pet me—

His teeth scrape across the sensitive tip of my breast and I gasp. He pauses, as if he wants to ask if I'm okay. But then he sucks me in again and I bite back a moan.

My hands tighten, my nails making indents in the wood.

If this were in any way a normal situation, I'd be sinking my hands into that dark mess of hair and pulling him even closer. My pussy clenches at the thought of how that hair will feel trailing over my skin.

Is it coarse or silky or somewhere in between?

His lips are lulling me into a state between dreams and reality, where the fact that I'm a thief and he's forcing me—

But he isn't using force. I had a choice. I could have left.

Instead, I'm naked, on his desk.

Some tidbit of information keeps trying to rise to the surface of my brain. Some fact that I can feel just out of my reach but my brain is so muddled right now, I can't focus.

He alternates between caresses and soft bites that make it even harder for me to breathe. He seems to be having no trouble at all.

Except... I feel his breath against my skin, a hard rush of air that raises goosebumps.

My pussy aches, already wet and throbbing, and my heart pounds.

I want to give myself over to the sensation, so new and amazing.

No other man has ever made me feel like this. Not one. My experience isn't huge. I've only ever been with three men in my life. And the first two don't count because one was a teenager who had even less of a clue than me and the other—

I shut off that train of thought when it threatens to open memories better left untouched. The third hadn't had a tenth of the skill this man possesses.

As if he senses my thoughts fragmenting, he lifts his head and stares into my eyes. I swallow hard, because that look demands more than I should be willing to give.

Except I am. Willing. And now I need to know.

"What's your name?"

The words come out barely above a whisper but I know he hears me. His expression doesn't change but his laser focus intensifies until I want to look away. But I don't.

"You rob my home but you don't know my name?"

Since the information meant nothing, I say, "I was only told what I needed was here. I have no idea who you are."

"And you want to know the name of the man who's going to make you come."

The way he says that word makes heat burst through my belly.

"I want to know your name."

His eyebrows rise slightly. "Sometimes we're doomed to disappointment, sweetheart."

The way he speaks makes that itch in the back of my brain start up again until finally I know what I need to ask.

"How do you know my name?"

He doesn't answer right away, just continues to stare at me until I can barely breathe.

"That's not the question you want answered, now, is it?"

I open my mouth to ask another question but he beats me to the punch.

"Lie back."

The lust that had been fading as questions rose roars back with a vengeance, but I refuse to give him anything more until I get something in return. I know it's stupid, considering the situation. I know I have absolutely no leverage. But I want his name.

"Tell me your name."

His eyes narrow and I hold my breath, waiting for him to kick me out, without that file.

He doesn't. He stares at me with hooded eyes, as if he's trying to decide how to handle me.

"I'll tell you my name and then I want to hear you scream it when you lie on your back and I lick you until you come."

Oh my god. I can't breathe. Air freezes in my lungs and I force myself to make them work. My breasts rise as I inhale and his gaze drops to watch them. The nipples tighten even more and the ache in the pit of my stomach intensifies. Moisture seeps from my pussy to slick my thighs.

His nostrils flare, as if he can smell my arousal. I watch

his throat convulse as he swallows and he moves an inch closer.

I involuntarily move backward an inch and his lips curl slightly.

He stays silent for another thirty seconds. "You can call me Aiden."

Whether that's his real name or not, I have no idea. But I like it.

Which is ridiculous. This whole situation is ridiculous.

But I'm following through because I have to. Some things are more important than what he wants from me.

He only wants my body. I can give him that. As long as I get what I need in return.

Aiden leans forward again and, this time, I don't retreat.

"Now that we've been introduced... Lie back, Olivia."

The desk is wide enough that my head doesn't fall off the other end. My body is so hot, the cool desk feels good against my back.

My gaze trained on that beautiful ceiling, I attempt to breathe normally. But anticipation beats in my blood. I can't see him but I know he hasn't moved away. The heat of his body singes my shins and my body tenses for his touch.

Just when I think he must have changed his mind, I feel a brief shift in the air before his hands land on my thighs.

I jerk, every muscle in my body tensing before I relax. But I can't control my breathing and hyperventilation becomes a distinct possibility.

"Frightened?"

His voice is so deep and raspy, I can't help but shiver.

"No."

"Then why are you shaking? You can walk out the door at any time."

"I'm not going anywhere."

His hands tighten almost imperceptibly on my thighs, as if I'd surprised him. Maybe I have. Maybe he expected me to leave. Is he trying to scare me off?

Hell, I should've run for the window and taken my chances. He probably would've caught me but at least I would've made a token effort.

What does he think of me?

Why do I even care?

His hands begin to exert pressure on my thighs to move them apart and now I resist, more out of stubbornness than anything.

I hear him huff, the sound amused, and my jaw tightens.

Damn him for making me want this, even though I shouldn't.

"Are you going to deny me now?"

His hands still and I want him to continue. Conflicting desires tear at me and my brain runs at breakneck pace, urging me to give him what he wants.

"No."

I make a conscious effort to relax my thighs but they continue to quiver as he slowly pushes them apart.

Cooler air brushes against the inside of my thighs and against the heated lips of my sex. The ache that's been growing inside me begins to spread. And when he speaks, I'm afraid I might embarrass myself completely and orgasm just from the sound.

"So pretty. Are you wet for me, or are you thinking of someone else right now, Olivia?"

I don't answer because I'm not sure I would make sense.

In my mind, I can see this totally surreal scene. Me spread on his desk, him staring down at me like a hawk.

I want to make him hurry, to get this over with. But another part of me wants him to drag this out all night. I want him to make me come over and over until I can't scream anymore and he's exhausted.

I should want him to fuck me fast so I can leave.

But no, I want everything.

"I'm going to put my fingers in your pussy and that's going to be your first orgasm." He sounds like he's having an everyday conversation. "Then I'm going to put my mouth on you and that'll be your second. Then I'm going to fuck you with my cock and play with your clit and make you come again. And then I'm going to flip you over and fuck you from behind so I can see that gorgeous ass."

The images he's creating in my brain are so erotic I gasp, but when his fingers finally touch me, I moan.

He moves closer until his hips are between my thighs, holding me open, as his fingers play along my folds. My sheath clenches and I want him to use those fingers to fill me, to fuck me. To give me some relief from this aching desire.

My back arches slightly as he slides in just the tips of

two fingers then retreats. The touch is only enough to make me want more.

The next time, his fingers slide a little farther, coating them with my wetness. As they sink deeper each time, he scissors them, working my tight muscles open, playing with me.

"So tight." His voice is barely audible in the silent room. "Christ, you're going to feel amazing around my cock."

I bite my bottom lip against the urge to encourage him to go harder and deeper. I shouldn't be enjoying this but I am and he knows it. But I don't have to feed his ego by begging.

On the next invasion, his fingers slide in as far as they'll go and everything goes black as I close my eyes. I'm trying not to hyperventilate but sensation riots through my body. I want to wrap my legs around his hips and bring him closer but I force them to remain down.

When he twists his hand and his fingers rub against my sensitive inner walls, I swallow a moan.

But he won't let me hold back. He withdraws then sinks his fingers deeper again. And when he flexes his hand, the tips of his fingers stroke me high inside, hitting a spot that makes me detonate.

I bite my lip to keep from crying out but I know he feels my contractions around his fingers.

He says something I don't hear because I'm breathing so hard and the blood is rushing in my ears. It takes me at least a minute to be able to breathe somewhat normally and to realize his fingers are still inside me, still stroking me. My body continues to respond, my pussy clenching around him, as if to keep him there.

Rational thought is no longer an option. He's replaced reality with dream.

I want him to continue. I need him to continue, to give me everything he promised.

I part my lips to breathe more deeply and I swear I can smell his arousal in the air. It's intoxicating. I want to put my mouth on his body and lick his skin.

Oh my god. There really must be something wrong with me.

Then again, he's played me perfectly. He's known exactly how to make my body do what he wants, how to steal my breath and my sanity.

I struggle to rise out of the haze he's laid over my mind. Shake my head and attempt to control my breathing.

And then he plants his free hand on the desk beside my hip and leans over me.

SIX

Olivia

MY BRAIN FLASHES red with warning. It's been doing that since Aiden and I started this...whatever this is.

I can't call it a game. There's too much on the line. It's more like cat-and-mouse. And the cat's about to devour me.

He's already had a taste and I barely survived. Now he wants to finish me off and I'm not sure I'll be the same when he's done. He's trying to goad me into giving him what he wants. If I don't, I don't get the file. If I do... What does that make me?

Horny as all hell, that's what. My body is more than willing. Each of the preceding orgasms have pushed me a little farther toward the edge of no return.

I'd already resigned myself to going over that edge but now... Now I realize I want to be pushed over. And I want him to do it...need him to do it.

Up until just a few seconds ago, I'd been telling myself I'd do whatever it took to get that file. Now I'm wondering if letting him fuck me is going to take me a step too far over a line I don't think I should cross.

Yes, I've already crossed so many tonight, what was one more? And yet...

I want him. These past two weeks, while I watched him, I've fallen for him. I hate to admit it, but I want him to want me like a man wants a woman. I also know that isn't going to happen here.

He's using me, just as I'm using him.

So let him use you and be done with it.

Except now he wants me to watch him stroke himself and this feels almost too personal. And how stupid is that? Too stupid to let it keep me from getting that file.

"No, I haven't lost my nerve." I meet his gaze again. "Go ahead. Stroke yourself. I'll watch."

Then I let my gaze fall and try not to swallow my tongue. His hand is huge, but it doesn't overshadow his cock. So that'll tell you how big his cock is. I mean, it's not grossly oversized, not long, but damn, is it thick. I swallow and try to calm my breathing but it's a losing cause.

Then his hand begins to move again and I'm transfixed. He begins slowly, dragging his palm and fingers along the shaft to just under the head then pulling back down. The head is a deep shade of red and the shaft is heavily veined. My fingers twitch, as if aching to touch him.

As he begins to move faster, I sneak a glance at his face and find him watching me, his eyes narrowed and focused on me. I can't maintain eye contact and let my gaze fall again to his fingers, now moving with more speed. I can't imagine he isn't hurting himself the way he pulls and tugs. I can never imagine handling him like he's treating himself.

Instead, I think about kneeling on the ground, putting my mouth over him and sucking him in. The thought makes me drag in a rough gasp, my fingers digging into the edges of the desk. I've almost forgotten I'm naked but now I remember and my thighs move restlessly against the wood.

My hands flex against the edge of the desk and my nails dig into the wood as he picks up even more speed. I wonder if he's going to make himself come, if he'll shoot over my stomach. I must be out of my mind because I don't want him to come anywhere but inside me. I want him to fuck me.

"If you make yourself come, do I still get the file?"

It was the only thing I could think to say to distract myself from the mesmerizing sight before me. I lift my gaze a second before his mouth quirks in a hard-edged grin.

"I'm not going to come until I'm so far inside you, you won't be able to breathe."

He looks deadly serious and I need to knock him down a peg. I can't let him get away with that.

"You can try."

That grin turns into a true smile, turning him even more devastatingly handsome than he already is.

"That's a dare you're going to lose."

Oh god, I hope so. "You have a pretty high opinion of yourself."

"I haven't had any complaints."

No, I bet he hasn't, under normal circumstances. But these aren't normal circumstances.

"Do all your deals include sex?"

If I think I can throw him off his game, I'm sadly mistaken.

"No. Only those where I find a beautiful woman sneaking into my house to steal from me."

"Technically, I was sneaking out."

I'm trying not to show my increasing desire for him but between the banter and the motion of his hand still wrapped around his cock, I'm sinking even further into lust and I'm afraid I'm going to lose myself.

"Semantics." His voice has deepened. "Now...grab the condom and put it on me."

I blink and suck in a sharp breath. Where the hell am I supposed to get—

"It's on the desk beside you."

I look to the left and there it is, a small square foil packet. I pick it up and hold it between us. When the hell had he put it there? How did I miss that? Uncertainty swamps me and I stare at that little packet for several long seconds. When I open this, my fate is sealed. It's the point of no return. I don't want to say no. I just wish...

What? That I'm not being blackmailed for sex by the man on whom I've developed an unhealthy obsession? That I'm not sitting on his desk naked for any reason other than the fact that he wants me?

"Olivia? Are you saying no?"

I look up, into his eyes. "What do you get out of this?

Are you a degenerate who gets off on having sex with women who can't say no?"

The words come out a little harsher than I'd planned. His eyes narrow again. I brace for a blow. I know how to take a hit.

He does nothing but stand there until, after several seconds, he takes a step away.

"You're free to leave. You have been this entire time. I'm not going to call the police. But you don't get to leave with the file."

I stay silent, watching him, trying to figure out what I should do. I really only have one option. I lift the condom between us and rip it open. His expression never changes but his jaw clenches. Had he been afraid I'd leave? Would he have cared?

"Put it on me."

The growl in his voice makes me think he would've been disappointed if I'd left. Or I'm projecting something that isn't there to justify my behavior when I really should be getting this over with so I can leave as soon as possible. And yet, I don't want it to be over so fast.

I've been holding his gaze for long seconds now, the torn foil wrapper in my hand. He hasn't moved, hasn't made a sound since he told me to put it on.

My gaze drops again and I let myself stare at his groin. He's no longer touching himself and I can see his cock, naked and straining toward me. I should walk out. Kick him in the balls now when he's least expecting it and run with the file.

A good thief does whatever it takes to get the prize. But I want to do him.

I want to finish this. I want my prize and I want him. Then I'll leave and never return. Never see him again.

I take the condom out of the packet and drop the packet on the desk. Then I sit up straighter, getting closer to him, and fit the condom to the head of his cock. His lungs contract and he sucks in an audible breath, the first sign, besides his erection, that he's affected by me.

It makes me bolder.

I roll the condom down his shaft, my fingers taking care to smooth and pet. I feel the heat of his skin through the latex, feel the pulsing blood beneath. The condom is lubricated and slick but I know he won't have any trouble entering me.

I'm wet and waiting. I only have to think about him fucking me and I get even wetter. I force myself to breathe deeply and get a shot of air laced with his scent. Nothing overpowering, just subtly male with an underlying hint of sandalwood. Masculine. Makes me want to lick his skin.

I swallow hard as my fingers finally reach the base of his cock. I pull back, put my hands back on the edge of desk, and stare directly into his eyes. His gaze is almost too intense to hold but I do.

"Tell me again, Olivia. Say it."

I know what he wants from me. At this point, I'm willing to give him anything he wants to make him fuck me. Except beg. I won't do that.

But I will say what he wants to hear. "Yes."

Without hesitation, he shoves one hand into my hair,

tilting my head back, and finally he puts his mouth over mine and kisses me. The shock of his lips taking mine steals my breath and I reach for his shoulders to push him away, just so I can breathe. He won't let me retreat more than a few centimeters but it's enough for me to fill my lungs.

As soon as I do, I feel the tip of his cock touch the lips of my sex, pushing between them, the pressure to part building as my hands on his shoulders hold him tight. I don't push him away but I don't try to drag him closer, either. I don't think I could even if I tried because he's controlling my every movement.

With his hands on my hips, he prevents me from tilting my pelvis forward, which I want to do to force his cock higher inside me. To give me more.

Instead, he goes slow and steady, his cock spreading my labia, making my sheath tighten and ache. Frustration builds from a pit in my stomach to a grinding ache between my thighs.

I lift my legs to wrap around his waist. He doesn't object or force them down so I tighten them, my heels digging into his ass, trying to pull him closer.

Instead, he pulls out, making me moan into his mouth. He takes the advantage to slide his tongue into my mouth and I suck on him, desperate for relief, to drive him crazy, make him as mad as I feel so that I can gain some ground here.

I swear I feel his mouth curve in a smile against mine and now I'm so damn horny and angry. Angry that he won't give me what I want. What I need.

I nip at his tongue. He pulls away, grinning outright now.

"Getting frustrated?"

His smile is not nice, but I don't want nice. I want dirty. And I want it now.

"Maybe I just want this to be over."

His grin widens even more. "Now that's an outright challenge. Because I don't want this to be over. At least not until the sun's shining high above the horizon."

I think of the hours between now and then, think of all we can do in that space of time, and I suck in air because, all of a sudden, I can't breathe.

"I'm going to take you on this desk and make you scream my name. Then I'm going to take you to that chair and you're going to ride me until you can't move and then I'll help you until I get off."

My gaze flicks to the chair where he'd been sitting and I see the image in my mind, exactly what he wants me to do. When I drag my gaze back to his, I lean closer.

"Then do it. Now."

Some emotion passes over his expression, but it's gone before I can decipher it. In the next second, he grabs my hips and pulls me forward and sinks deep. The abrupt intrusion is a shock to my system, and I gasp, my brain short-circuiting at the sense of fullness. My hands slap on his shoulders, though I'm not sure whether I'm pulling him closer or pushing him away. Maybe both.

My nose is centimeters from his chest, still covered by his t-shirt. I want to rub the tip against his chest but I want skin-on-skin contact. I'm not sure if I can form a coherent sentence, while his cock is deep inside me...not deep enough. I'm hanging on to my control by a thread. And I want him to lose the shirt.

I let my hands slide from his shoulders down his biceps, hear his breath hiss in through his teeth. He's not as untouchable as he appears. My hands continue down to his waist while he holds steady inside me. If the situation weren't so surreal, I would laugh. But I'm so turned on, all I can do is focus on one thing at a time.

Now, I want him as exposed as I am.

I slip my hands under the hem of his tight black t-shirt and swallow hard as my palms land on bare skin. Hot to the touch and sleek. I run my fingers up his abs, rigid and defined. I'd seen him walk through the house many times in the past week without the shirt and I'd fantasized about touching him. About licking my way up those abs and teasing his nipples with my tongue and teeth, like he'd done to me.

My body tightens around him at the thought. He groans, his body tensing. He takes a step closer and inches me forward and now he's buried as deep as he can possibly be, my thighs spread wide and my legs wrapped around his waist.

My obsession with taking his shirt off grows until I grab the hem and tug it up. For a few seconds, I don't think he's going to let me strip it off. Finally, he releases my hips and helps me get it over his head.

My mouth waters at the sight. This close, it's so much more enticing. I lift my hands to stroke his pecs, covered lightly with dark hair. Aiden doesn't manscape, and damn if that isn't sexier than any shaved and oiled model ever could be.

He stills at my touch and I play my fingers over his nipples, tight and pointed and nearly hidden. I brush the hair out of my way then lean forward to put my mouth on him.

I tease the tip of my tongue over his nipples and his hands settle on my shoulders, fingers tightening until I know I wouldn't be able to get away unless he allows it. But I'm not going anywhere until he gives me what I want. And I don't just mean the file.

There's a subtle shift in the mood between us. I can't explain it, and, at the moment, I don't care. I only know he needs to feel a bit of the same wildness he's raised in me.

While I play my tongue against his nipples, I stroke my hands around to his back and slide my fingers beneath the waistband of his jeans. He's only pushed them down far enough to release his cock, now hot and hard inside me. I push them down even farther so I can put my hands on his ass. I pet him, squeeze him, and lightly tease the crease between his cheeks, which makes him growl low in his chest.

Power sweeps through me and I know, at that moment, I could do whatever I want to him and he wouldn't complain—

He pulls back and thrusts forward, stealing my breath and my concentration. And making my body shake and contract around him. My gaze flashes up and locks with his. I see the wildness there I hadn't before. A muscle jumps in his tight jaw.

"You're going to want to hold on."

I don't get to say anything because he repeats his actions, pulling out until only the tip remains inside then shoving forward with a controlled thrust and sinking deep.

My arms automatically go around his shoulders, arching my back to press my chest against his, as if he's going to provide me with stability. But no, he wants to strip whatever stability I have left.

"Look at me while I fuck you, Olivia. I want to see your eyes. I want to drown in them. And I want you to drown with me."

I'm already halfway there and it won't take much to push me under completely.

Every word he says sends a shiver through my body as I ache from his intrusion. I want him to move. I want him to fuck me hard and fast, but I want what he promised. To take me all night long.

I don't want this to be over because when it is...

When it is, I'll have to face reality.

Another withdrawal but this time he pushes in so slowly, I swear I can't breathe. My sex draws him in, milks him. Every breath I take is laced with his scent and I swear it makes me high.

"Faster."

My voice is barely above a whisper, but I know he hears me because his beautiful lips curves into that rough smile that makes my stomach twist and turn like I'm on a roller coaster.

"No."

He pulls out again, even slower than before. I can feel

every bump and ridge and I hate the intrusion of the condom. That's how far gone I am. And I just don't care. I lift one hand from his shoulder and wrap it in his hair as he tilts his pelvis and works his way back inside.

I tug, not caring if it hurts. He can take a little pain. He can probably take a lot.

"Yes."

He seats his cock deep again and I feel the hair at his groin tickle against my sex. "You're in no position to demand anything. In fact, I think you need to be reminded where your place is. Lie back, Olivia. I want to watch you."

I freeze. If I lie back, I'll be completely exposed. And I won't be able to touch him. I won't be able to anchor myself.

"Lie back."

I shake my head. "No."

"I'll make it worth your while. Do it, Olivia."

There's a request in his tone, but there's also a demand and I freeze. He puts his hands on my shoulders and presses me back. He doesn't force and I go, reluctantly, until I'm staring at the ceiling, and my body is trembling almost violently.

I don't know why I'm having this reaction, don't know why every sensation is suddenly intensified. But now I'm lying here shaking and waiting for him to move.

When he finally does, thrusting forward with a little more force, I'm shocked. And so damn aroused, I'm already halfway to another orgasm.

Another thrust and I can't contain a gasp.

He stops, his hips pressed against my thighs, spreading me open, exposing me.

"Am I hurting you?"

He sounds as if he's gritting his teeth, holding himself back. I shiver at the restrained emotion in his voice, wondering what would happen if he let himself go.

Part of me wants to push him past that restraint. Part of me wants him to finish so I can leave. A very small part, if I'm honest.

Because, honestly, I've never felt more alive than I do right at this moment. My life is so restricted, so constrained. But here, now, I feel like I'm not me. I'm someone else whose life won't be completely upended by this act when I leave.

And I will leave and never see this man again.

In answer to his question, I raise my arms over my head, grab the opposite edge of the desk to brace myself, then tighten my legs and bring him even closer.

Drawing my gaze from the ceiling, I look into his eyes.

"Do it. Fuck me. Now."

SEVEN

Olivia

I CAN BARELY BREATHE. My heart pounds against my ribs like a trapped bird and I'm pretty sure I might actually hyperventilate.

I'm fighting to take slow, deep breaths but I'm losing the battle. Every breath I draw in smells like him. He's still pulsing inside my body, and he has me pressed against his chest so tightly, I feel his heart thumping against mine.

The intimacy of the situation is fucking with my head and I'm actually arguing with myself about how right this feels. The rational part of my brain knows this situation isn't right. This situation is so far from normal, it's practically psychotic.

And yet...I don't want to leave. That's the most insane thought I've had all night.

Panic works its way back into my system and he must

be able to tell because his arms tighten even more. The false sense of security helps to calm my heart rate but after several long seconds, reality seeps in.

I've completed my part of the bargain. It's time to get what I came for and leave. Before he can convince me to stay any longer. It wouldn't be that hard.

I freeze for a second before I begin to pull away. His arms don't release me right away and a part of me wants to smile in triumph. The rest of me realizes I'm being ridiculous and puts a little more effort into my escape.

It's going to be awkward getting off the chair, considering his cock is still lodged inside me. And even though he's softening, he's still big enough to make me feel stretched.

Heat burns my cheeks and, for a second, I don't know what to do. Then he takes the decision out of my hands. He releases his arms and uses one hand to hold the condom at the base of his cock and the other to help me stand.

My gaze falls to his groin, and I watch as he takes off the condom then knots it. His fingers twist and my pussy clenches against the remembered feel of them stroking inside me.

He's so close, my nose practically brushes against his chest and if I wanted to, I could stick my tongue out and lick him.

His skin would taste warm and a little salty. And I'd be tempted to bite him—

I take a step away and nearly stumble. He reaches for me, one hand wrapping around my upper arm to keep me from tipping over. I flinch, and he immediately releases me. I want his hand back.

Turning with a jerk, I search for my clothes. Suddenly, I desperately need to be covered. I see clothing strewn all over the floor. My pants, my shirt, my bra. I grab them then I force myself to slow down.

I can't fall apart now. I'll have more than enough time when I get home to examine every second of this night. But right now, I have to hold it together long enough to get what I came for and leave.

I pull on my pants, forgoing underwear because I don't see my panties and I'm not going to take the time to look for them. I pull my shirt over my head without my bra, which I stuff in my pants pocket. I mark the location of my shoes then take a deep breath and turn.

He's pulled on his jeans but not his shirt and he's sitting in the chair again. More like sprawled, as he was in the desk chair. His hair, almost as long as mine, spills over his shoulders and my fingers curl with the desire to sink into it. Then my gaze locks on to his bare chest and my mouth waters.

Oh my god, this is insane. I should want to run like hell. After I get that file, of course. Instead, I stand here thinking about going down on my knees and sucking his cock into my mouth and making him groan.

Shaking my hair over my shoulders, I force myself to stare into his eyes.

"I've fulfilled my part of the bargain. Give me the file."

He doesn't answer right away, and he doesn't move.

Instead, his gaze travels down my body, as if reassessing now that he's seen me naked.

My chin lifts and I gain a little steel in my backbone.

"Maybe I'm not satisfied."

His voice rasps across my raw senses and it takes a second for his meaning to sink in. And when it does, two thoughts spring to mind.

Bastard.

And...

More.

Jaw tight, I cross my arms over my chest.

"That wasn't part of the deal."

He shrugs, looking so hard and uncaring, a sliver of fear stabs me in the gut.

"I don't care. And you're not in much of a position to argue."

He's absolutely right. White noise fills my head as I stare at the man who holds the life of my father in his hands. And I realize he knows exactly who I am and why I'm here. What I don't know is why.

My gaze narrows. "Who are you?"

He doesn't answer right away, just continues to watch me with that stone-faced expression. A chill crawls up my back and my stomach begins to churn. I've been played. I don't know how or why but I do know I fucked up somewhere.

Now I'm trapped.

Fight-or-flight kicks in, the rush of adrenaline burning like acid through my veins. My first instinct is to run. My second is to smack his face.

"You're going to have to discover that on your own."

The ice in his voice makes me want to punch him. My hands clench into fists at my sides as his mouth curls into a hard grin.

Slowly, he rises from his chair and walks to the desk. I'm not sure I can stand to look at it now. I'm afraid I might puke.

Jesus, how stupid have I been?

At the desk, he grabs the file I'd tried to steal and holds it in front of him, his gaze boring into mine.

"I'm willing to give you part of what you need tonight."

His words don't make sense right away but he continues as my mind races, trying to catch up.

"Consider it a down payment. But I've decided I'm not finished with you. Come back two nights from now. Use the front door this time."

My mouth drops open as stunned disbelief blankets my brain.

"And if I say no?"

It's a stupid question but I can't help myself. I know I'm caught but I also know I can't give up without a fight.

His expression doesn't change. "I'm pretty sure you know exactly what happens."

And so does he. I can see it in his eyes. Jesus. I walked into a trap I never saw coming. I've been so damn stupid. There's no other answer I can give.

"I agree."

EIGHT

Olivia

"OH MY GOD, Livvie, you've been gone forever. Are you okay? What happened? Where have you been all this time? Are you hurt?"

Maylyn grabs my arm as soon as I open the front door, pulling me into our dad's house and slamming the door shut behind me.

So much for sneaking in to talk to Dad without her finding out.

"I'm fine." I nod and smile and hope like hell my expression doesn't give away my lie. There's no way I'm telling her what happened last night. I can barely wrap my head around it. "I'm just tired."

"I can see that."

Maylyn gives me a thorough once-over, and if I didn't know better, I'd swear she can see exactly what happened in the past few hours written on my face. Which is ridiculous, I know. I just need to hold myself together for a little while longer.

But it's getting harder with every second.

I barely remember walking back to my car from the mansion. I know I spent a few minutes simply trying to catch my breath, my hands wrapped around the steering wheel until they hurt. When I finally thought I could drive home without causing an accident, I turned the key and drove away, hyperaware of everything around me.

I'd considered going straight to my apartment and falling into bed, avoiding my dad for a little while longer. But I knew he'd be pacing the floors waiting for me, and he deserves to know what happened as soon as possible.

I'd hoped Maylyn would be gone by the time I got here. Apparently, I have absolutely no luck today. Unless you count multiple orgasms lucky.

Maylyn's forehead crinkles and her lips flatten into a straight line as she continues to stare, looking much older than her twenty years.

Damn it, I never should've told her I was going last night. But she's my sister, the only person in whom I confide everything. Except what happened last night.

"Where's Dad?"

Maylyn rolls her eyes. "I'm sure he'll be here in a second. Tell me what—"

"Did you get it?"

I turn to see my dad in the doorway that leads to the living room. Hands stuffed in the pockets of his jeans, Patrick Maloney stares at me with eyes the same blue as

Maylyn's, wearing the concert t-shirt she and I bought him the last time he took us to see Slipknot.

He's fifty but usually looks a decade younger. This morning, he looks like he's aged twenty years. He must be able to tell from my face that I have bad news because his eyes close slowly, and he sucks in a deep breath. And the hole in my gut becomes a crater.

I swallow and try not to think about how I traded sex for the paper in my pocket, how I promised to return tomorrow night for more of both. I try to concentrate on the fact that I'm helping my dad get the information he needs to keep him and Maylyn safe.

"I have part of what we need but...not all of it. I'm going to get the rest. I just need some time."

Dad's eyes fly open, and he pins me with a look I remember from my childhood, what my siblings and I call his x-ray vision.

"What does that mean? What happened?"

There's no way in hell I'm going to tell the man who raised me that the man I tried to rob last night made me come multiple times on top of his desk. There're some things you just don't tell your dad. Or your brothers. If they ever find out, they'll hunt Aiden down and kill him. Slowly.

And they're good enough to get away with it. If my dad weren't being threatened to provide the information Aiden holds, I might actually let them.

Are you sure about that?

"It means I ran into a complication and wasn't able to get everything." My sister gasps and my dad's mouth opens, but I continue before they can speak. "But I have a plan to get the rest. We have until the end of next week. I'll have everything we need by then. I swear."

Silence holds for about two seconds before Maylyn's questions pour out of her like water.

"What complication? What happened? Are you hurt?"

But it's my dad's silence that holds my attention.

We may not share any genes, but he's been my father since I was three years old. Until I was fifteen, I believed he was my biological father. He probably never would've told me otherwise if I hadn't overheard Bryant and Reese talking about how they'd found me.

It had rocked the foundation of my world, and Reese still feels guilty as hell. And yeah, there are days I wish I'd never found out. But I've never once felt my dad has treated me any differently than Maylyn.

Sure, some people think he trained me to follow in his footsteps because I'm not biologically his. What they don't know is he tried his damnedest to stop me. Until he realized he couldn't. Then he trained me to be a damn good cat burglar who'd never been caught...until last night.

"Livvie! Oh my god." Maylyn grabs my arm, drawing my attention back to her. "Are you listening to me? What the hell happened?"

My sister stops long enough to take a breath and my dad finally speaks.

"You got caught."

My cheeks flush and Maylyn gasps, her hold on my arm tightening.

"What? Are you okay? How did you get away? What happened? Who—"

Dad lays a hand on my sister's shoulder and her mouth snaps shut.

"Are you hurt?" His voice is tight, and I hear his fear.

I shake my head emphatically. "No, I'm not hurt. I wasn't injured. And no, I wasn't caught. I made a miscalculation about the mark's schedule, which means I had to make some adjustments to my plan. But I was able to get some of what you need before I had to leave."

I'd rehearsed what I was going to say the entire ride home. I'd only had forty-five minutes to do it, but I think I came up with something plausible. Now I just have to sell it.

I pull the paper out of my pocket and give it to my dad. He doesn't take it right away. He's trying to figure out if I'm lying and, if I am, about what.

But I am damn good at lying. And there's no way in hell I'm going to tell him I fucked a stranger for that information.

Or that you enjoyed it.

Heat burns beneath my skin. Yes, I did enjoy it. And I will take that secret to my grave.

All my dad needs to know now is that I will get the rest of what he needs. That's all anyone needs to know, Maylyn included.

After several seconds, he takes a shaky breath, looks down at the paper, and scans it. Some of the lines on his face disappear. But not all.

"I'll have the rest by the end of next week." I reach for

Maylyn's hand and squeeze. "Don't worry. This'll all be over soon."

Maylyn shrugs, dismissing my fear for her in a heartbeat. But the look I exchange with Dad is tense. Only he and I know the truth. That if I don't get what he needs, his life will be forfeit.

A local crime boss with a grudge against my dad is threatening to make him an example of what happens when you fail him. He's promised to make dad's death slow and painful. And that when he is done with Dad, he'll start on my brothers and work his way down to me and Maylyn.

I only know all of this because Vincenzo, a snake in a five-thousand-dollar suit, used me to get the message to my dad.

"I'm not worried about me," Maylyn says with a huff. "You're the one breaking and entering and stealing. I'm just the one sitting home worrying."

"Well, you don't have to worry because I'm fine." I roll my eyes and spread my arms wide. "I'm here. I'm not going anywhere. But you are. Don't you have school this morning? Isn't Raj here yet?"

The classmate who picks up Maylyn for school every day is rarely late. He's paid well not to be. Of course, Maylyn has no idea Dad pays the son of a local gang member to keep her safe during the day at the local college where she's enrolled. She thinks they're friends. Good friends. And they are. But like everything else in our lives, there's the truth and then there's the version of the truth we tell each other.

Maylyn huffs and shakes her head, but at that moment,

a car beeps from the street out front. My sister's jaw sets, and I see frustration in the lines on her forehead. Better that than outright horror at what I've done.

She points at me, her mouth set in a pout that gets her out of almost any trouble. Not that she ever really gets in trouble. She's practically perfect. Straight-A student. A sweetheart with a heart of gold and a smile that lights up a room. My brothers and my dad and I like to pretend we can keep her that way. But short of locking her in her room for the rest of her life, I know that's not going to happen.

So far, we've managed to keep her out of the family business, insulated from the more illegal aspects of our lives.

"We are so not done with this conversation." She shakes her head and sighs. "And if I didn't have a chem test, I'd stay home and force you to tell me."

With a flounce I've never perfected, even when I was a teen, she grabs her backpack off the chair and opens the door, turning to glare at me. "You are *so* hiding something, and I'm going to find out what it is."

Then she shuts the door behind her and I'm alone with Dad, whose gaze has dropped to the paper.

"Is that at least part of what you need?"

He doesn't answer right away, and fear knots my stomach. Oh my god, what if Aiden played me? What if he gave me dummy information? What if—

"Yeah, it is." Sighing, Dad shakes his head, and I mentally prepare myself for his disappointment. But before I can apologize, his gaze narrows. "Damn it, Livvie, what the hell happened? Are you really okay?"

I'm not. I want to retreat to my apartment and sleep so I can forget the past hours. Or be alone so I can relive them. But like I said, I'm a damn good liar.

"I'm fine. I'm tired, I need a shower and some food, but I'm fine, Dad. Seriously."

He stares at me for what seems like an hour, and I almost convince myself he can read my mind. If he could, I'm pretty sure he'd be halfway to Aiden's place with the Berretta stashed in his bedside table.

Yes, my dad is a thief. Like me, he's a damn good one. But Patrick Maloney instilled in me a code of conduct he doesn't always adhere to himself. And yeah, I know how that sounds. Most people grow up with their parents telling them, "Don't steal. It's wrong."

I grew up in a family where "stealing" isn't always "wrong." Growing up, stealing was the difference between starving and simply going to bed hungry. Or spending the night on the streets and having a roof over your head.

My dad has always done what needs to be done to make sure we had food and a bed. I have never doubted his love for me, my brothers or my sister. And if three of his four children followed in his footsteps... Well, my brothers and I are nonviolent. That doesn't mean we won't defend ourselves. It just means we have a certain...moral fluidity when it comes to making money.

I can see in his eyes he doesn't want to let this go, but there's no way in hell I'm telling him anything more. Finally, he takes a deep breath and releases it on a sigh.

"How are you going to get the rest?"

I make sure I continue to hold his gaze. "I made a deal. If I stick to it, he'll give me the rest of the information."

Dad frowns. "What deal? With who?"

"The man who lives in the house. When I fulfill my end of the bargain, I'll get the rest of the file."

He's silent for several seconds before he starts to pace.

"So you did get caught." Dad runs a hand through his already disheveled hair. "Damn it. I knew I shouldn't have involved you in this."

"I didn't give you a choice. And you know I'm better than you at lifting. Besides, I don't think this guy would've made a deal with anyone else."

He stops in front of me and that look's back in his eyes. "What exactly do you have to do to fulfill the deal?"

I'd tried to rehearse what I'd say when Dad asked this question, had come up with multiple answers. I give him the easiest. "I have to go back to the house tomorrow night. He wants me to do something for him in exchange for the information." *He wants to fuck me again.* "I do it and I leave with more pieces of the file."

"Do what exactly?"

I hold his gaze and lie. "I don't know yet. I think he wants me to steal something for him. Won't be the first time I've bartered services."

I can practically see the gears working in Dad's head, He looks me up and down again, as if he knows there's something I'm hiding, and he can find the clues on my body. Or he's looking for injuries.

Finally, his gaze meets mine again. "What did he want to know last night? And how the hell did you get away with this," he waves the paper in his hand, "and not the rest?"

"I told you. We made a deal."

He pauses for a few moments. "Does he know who you are? Know your name?"

"I gave him my first name. And he told me his. Aiden."

I see no recognition on my dad's face but, like I said, he's good.

"I want the surveillance photos you took." Dad straightens, and I see the man who's pulled off more jobs by the time he was twenty than I probably ever will. "All of them. I want to know who this guy is before you go back tomorrow."

I cross my arms over my chest, trying to ease the growing ache beneath my ribs. "I've tried to identify him for two weeks. I found nothing."

Dad's expression doesn't change. "Then you didn't look hard enough, and you don't have my resources. Get me the pictures immediately when you get home."

The demand in his voice is clear and I nod, wanting to avoid any more questions. I almost can't believe he's going to let me off the hook so easily, but I want to get back to my apartment and sleep for the next few hours. And hope like hell I don't dream about last night.

Closing the distance between us, he reaches out to cup my cheek and I see in his eyes the fear he hides from my sister.

"I'm not sending you back there until we know who this guy is and what he wants. And I want one of your brothers to shadow you."

God, what a disaster that would be. I shake my head. "No way. Reese and Bryant are as subtle as bulls in a china shop. I go alone. That's the deal I made, and I'm sticking to it. If you find out who he is before tomorrow night, fine. If not, it doesn't matter. I'm going back. But right now, I need some sleep. Trust me. I want to know who he is as much as you do so I'm going to go home and sleep for a few hours and then I'll figure out who he is."

He pauses for a second then shakes his head and sighs again. "I do trust you, Liv. You and Maylyn and your brothers are the only people I trust."

Family first. Always. The five of us against the world. It's been drilled into my head for as long as I can remember. I understand. Dad's been burned before. He's been used. And he's taken hits for crimes that weren't his. He's cleaned up a couple of my messes, and he's kept my brothers out of jail more than a few times.

"I know, Dad. But I'm dead on my feet right now. Let me get some sleep, then we can figure this out. Okay?"

He scowls, not happy, but finally he nods and rubs his hand over my head, as if I'm still ten years old. I roll my eyes because he'd be disappointed if I didn't. But his answering smile is worried.

"All right, sweetheart. Get some sleep and then I want you back here for dinner. Bring the surveillance photos. I'll see if your brothers can stop by, and we can hash this out together, figure out a strategy."

Oh goodie. Just what I need. Two more overprotective alpha males ready to defend my honor to the death.

"Dad, I don't—"

"Your brothers need to know what's going on." He grimaces and shoves a hand through his dark hair again. "At least some of what's going on. Damn it, I never should've involved you in this."

He hadn't wanted to. I'd volunteered then practically twisted his arm to get him to agree.

"Seriously, you're getting yourself worked up over nothing. Just stop. Everything's going to be okay. By the end of next week, we'll have everything you need to get Vincenzo off your back and we'll put all of this behind us."

My dad owes Marco Vincenzo. Vincenzo had hired him to do a job, a job that'd gone wrong. A robbery that should've been a cake walk and turned into a nightmare. I still don't know why he took it. Dad had graduated from petty B&E to become one of the very few thieves legitimate businesses trusted to do their dirty work. He'd built a reputation on clean, untraceable work that cost corporations money but not lives.

The fact that he'd taken a job for one of the most infamous crime bosses in Philadelphia didn't make any damn sense. And since he refused to explain, I can only take him on faith and do what I can to help.

Now, Dad looks at me as if he's trying to read my mind then forces something that looks like a smile, but it's gone in a flash.

"You're right. It'll be over soon. And then we can get the hell away from here."

For the past year or so, he's been talking about moving, somewhere smaller, somewhere warmer, where he can buy a business and "live like normal people." Since our lives have never been normal, I have no idea how "normal people" live. I do know I'd be bored stupid working behind a desk or a store counter or whatever else people do to make money to eat.

So would my brothers. And so would Dad. He'd be looking for his next adventure in less than a month. We know because we're exactly the same. Adrenaline junkies.

Which occasionally lands us in situations like the one I'm in now. Where there's no easy way out. If I'm honest, at least with myself, I might not want a way out. Maybe I want to go back to that mansion in the woods and see what else Aiden has in store for me.

Because for the first time in years, I'm excited about what the future holds.

NINE

Aiden

I HEAR the door close behind Olivia and my first instinct is to drag her back into the house, lay her out on the bed upstairs, and fuck her until neither of us can walk. Since I have enough sense to realize this would be treacherously close to the very thin line I'm walking as it is, I manage to keep myself in the chair until I know she's too far gone for me to catch.

My muscles ache by the time I head for my bedroom to shower and dress for the office. I briefly consider working from home, but if I stay here, I'll be climbing the walls in an hour. Better to get out.

Away from that damn desk.

Why the hell had I fucked her there? Now every time I sit behind it, I'll see Olivia spread out naked across it. Hell, just thinking about it now makes me hard. I want her again. Wanting her is a weakness I can't afford. So why the hell am I second-guessing every damn little thing?

Stop with the melodramatics. Don't allow anything to get in your way. Take what you want.

Sound advice, even if it was from my dad. The bastard had been a thorn in my side since Granddad had stepped down as the head of Squire Incorporated two years ago and named me his successor. He'd known his son would've run the empire into the ground but he hadn't wanted to cut my father out entirely. Which is why I can't get rid of the bastard. And I've tried. He's always lurking on the edges, looking for whatever advantage he can get.

The problem is, Mark Battle still holds enough power to be a massive pain in my ass. He's the public face of the company, the legitimate heir. I'm merely his bastard son. But his presence allows me to stay behind the scenes, where I can work without obstruction.

My father enjoys the spotlight. Thrives in it. avoid it whenever possible. I don't like the glad-handing and the fake smiles and the backstabbing. He loves playing king. Luckily for the health of the company, I make all the business decisions. He just needs to smile and look good in the pictures for the Wall Street Journal and Forbes.

I prefer designing things, building things. Keeping my identity secret allows me to do that without all the bullshit getting in the way. It means I can go to job sites in a hard hat and jeans and blend in without people trying to kiss my ass. Granddad made me see that being invisible is an asset. It's why he'll never acknowledge me as his grandson. I'm his secret weapon.

With my libido firmly shoved back into the dark hole where I normally keep it, I shower and dress, slam down three cups of coffee, and head out the door.

In seconds, I'm on my way to my office in Center City Philadelphia. But I'm already planning to make a stop first. I'm positive Oliva headed straight to Patrick Maloney's home to give him the information I'd given her. But I'm not going to follow her there. I don't want to take the chance she'll see me anywhere near her father's place.

She's too smart not to realize there's much more going on here than Vincenzo's simple blackmail plot. Hell, she might actually figure out who I am by the time she returns to my home tomorrow night. She's got a vested interest in knowing my name now.

And when she does? Will she still be willing to fuck me to save her father?

My jaw clenches and I want to punch something but since I can't exactly walk up to Maloney and punch him in the face...

No, Vincenzo set everything in motion exactly as I'd told him to. Now I need to let this play out. But I'd already screwed up because I changed the damn plan when I told her to come back tomorrow night.

And I don't regret that one damn bit.

Again, my mind conjures images from last night. At this rate, I'm going to have an erection all fucking day. My obsession with Olivia is growing and that's dangerous. I can't let it get out of hand. Can't allow it to go that far.

I'll sate myself with her then I'll move on. Her father will be destroyed. And after what Maloney took from my family, revenge will be sweet. And brutal. There's no help for that. My grandmother's death is on his head. Maloney deserves every bit of what's coming.

Olivia doesn't. Neither does her sister.

Fuck that. I knew going in there'd be collateral damage. And Olivia's no saint. Her list of crimes goes back almost a decade. Maylyn...

She's the only innocent in this whole mess. When this is over, I'll be sure she's taken care of. A scholarship to finish school. A job with the right company. Maybe I'll even tell Maloney who'll be responsible for his daughter's good fortune before Vincenzo takes him out. A final nail in his coffin.

Olivia will either drag herself through this. Or she won't. I won't care. If Granddad taught me anything, it's that I can't let emotion rule my actions. It's a sure way to get fucked. And not in a good way. Lust isn't an emotion. It's a bodily function. The need for sex is primal, like the need to eat and breathe. My desire to fuck Olivia means nothing other than I need to get laid and my body wants hers.

So why the hell am I planning to make a detour on my way to the office? I'm usually good at ignoring shit I don't want to deal with. Right now... My usual cool head isn't prevailing. It's the smaller head in my pants that's running the show.

Luckily, traffic sucks, as always, and I have to keep my attention on the road or risk getting sideswiped by a semi or rear-ended by a sedan. I've got a headache by the time I reach Fairmount Park and my temples throb with every car horn. I have the urge to throttle every other fucking driver in the city but when I finally reach my destination and park along the street, it's quiet.

This section of the neighborhood is blue-collar, with a couple of garages, including her brothers', and a few warehouses and businesses. Not many people live here, and those who do don't tend to hang on front porches and shoot the shit with their neighbors after work. Most of the residents in this neighborhood keep to themselves because they all have something to hide. Like Olivia and her brothers.

Her dad and younger sister live a few blocks away, in a more residential area. Nice house but nothing fancy in a working-class neighborhood where people don't have typical nine-to-five jobs. They come and go at all times.

Perfect place for a criminal to hide in plain sight.

I don't see Olivia's car outside her building, but she typically parks in the garage at the end of the street next to her brothers' auto-body shop. She's probably already inside and asleep.

Which is where I should be. Home and asleep. But I do have work that needs to be done and I need a clear head to do it. I should get to the office. Instead, I sit here for the next half hour, watching traffic. Finally, a flash of black in the rearview catches my eye, and I see her walking up the street.

She's still wearing the clothes she left my home in and hasn't braided her hair. It blows around her face in inky black strands that make my fingers tighten around the steering wheel. I want to wrap that hair around my hand

and pull her up against my body until there's no space between us. I want her to look up at me with that hint of defiance and breathless anticipation.

I want her to gasp when I push inside her, watch her try to hold back her reaction as I start to move.

Fuck. I'm hard again and I have no one to blame but myself. I should've stayed the fuck away from her. Maybe I am obsessed. Maybe I should've ended this game last night. Should've sent her back to her father in tears, spirit broken. Instead, I'm thinking of all the things I want to do to her tomorrow night. I wonder if she's thinking the same.

She looks lost in thought, head down. Christ, she's practically got a sign on her back that reads "Mug me."

Not that anyone would dare touch her if they know who she is. Her brothers would kill them. If they knew I'd fucked her, they'd probably cut off my balls and make me eat them before they put me out of my misery.

I will not feel sorry for last night. Her father deserves exactly what's coming to him. It's just too bad for her that she's the delivery method.

Yeah, right. Last night was not only about revenge.

Seconds later, she opens the door and disappears inside. Nothing more to see here. Except it takes me a full minute to turn the key and drive away.

I head downtown. Squire Incorporated maintains offices in a Walnut Street high-rise owned by one of its many shell companies. JP Holdings may be written on the door, but the actual business that goes on behind the door has nothing to do with real estate.

"Hello, Mr. Knight. I wasn't expecting to see you today."

"I wasn't expecting to be here today, Ms. Rodriguez. Anything I need to know?"

My personal assistant stands behind her desk, pushing a mass of brown curls over her shoulder as she reaches for a pile of papers. Everything else about Jeannie Rodriguez is perfectly pressed, from her straight black skirt to her white button-down shirt. Except for that hair. She can pull it back in a bun or a braid, but it never fails to find a way to escape.

It's like part of her needs to be rebellious.

"I was going to forward these to you later this morning, but since you're here, you can look them over and let me know if there's anything you need me to handle."

It's a rhetorical question because something always needs attention. When you oversee an operation as large and diverse as this one, there's always a crisis. Jeannie has been my personal assistant for five years and, in that time, she's learned how to prioritize, how to tell what's about to become a three-alarm fire and what can be passed on to the very few men I trust to handle high-level company business.

Granddad never let anyone handle his business but as the company has grown, I've needed help and there are only four men in the world I trust to handle what I throw at them. And one woman, though she wants nothing to do with the business.

I take the stack of papers from her hand. "Thank you. Let me know if anything else comes up."

"Are you going to be here for lunch?"

"Yes." And since I'm starving, I know exactly what I want. "Cheesesteaks."

Her lips quirk but she doesn't allow herself to smile. "Geno's or Pat's?"

I huff because this is a long-running battle. "You already know the answer to that."

She manages to roll her eyes respectfully. She's been with me long enough to know what she can and can't get away with. Her mother taught her well.

"Yes, sir. Pat's. Again. Do you need anything else right now? Coffee, maybe?"

"Do I look like I need it?"

She doesn't answer my question specifically, which is an answer in itself.

"I'll bring you a cup before I get back to work."

Jeannie turns and walks out, closing the door behind her. I turn to stare at the city spread out before me. I'd been born in Chicago, but after my mom dumped me on my dad's doorstep when I was ten, my dad dumped me here with Granddad and went back to his legitimate family in New York City.

Luckily, Granddad took me in, sent me to school, and eventually taught me how to run the company to prepare for the day he couldn't. That day had come two years ago. My grandfather handed over control of Squire Incorporated and he'd made me promise not to let my father blow it all. Or to allow the man who'd tried to ruin it get away with the crime.

Patrick Maloney needs to be taken care of. And now is the time.

TEN

Olivia

I DROP into bed seconds after I get home from my dad's and sleep for six solid hours. No dreams, no tossing or turning.

I wake around five in the afternoon and head straight for the shower, where I stand for at least fifteen minutes, letting scalding water pour over my body. My body aches, especially my arms and calves, sore from the climb.

My thighs...

I shake my head, trying to get the images to dislodge. I have a feeling that's going to take more than a hot soak. When I finally force myself out of the shower, I throw on boxer shorts and a tank top and head for the living area of my apartment.

And stop with a huff when I see my brother Reese sprawled on my couch, watching TV. I can only see the back of his head, but I know it's him and not Bryant because his hair is the same shade as Maylyn's and not the red-tinged brown of Dad's and Bryant's.

"Glad you made yourself comfortable." I continue into the room, rubbing a towel over my still-wet hair. "Did you raid my fridge too?"

Eyes glued to the TV, Reese lifts the bottle of flavored water and the sandwich in his hands high enough that I can see them over the couch. So that's a yes.

"How'd the job go last night?"

He speaks through a mouthful of food, and I roll my eyes even though he can't see me. Tossing my damp towel at his head, I ignore him and head for the kitchen. I need coffee if I'm going to have to deal with him.

"Goddammit, brat. I just asked a question. No need to get pissy about it."

I'm not pissy. I just don't want to have to talk to my older brother about last night. Even more than my dad and my sister, Reese sees what I don't want him to. If he finds out about the deal I made, Aiden won't just end up dead from a knife in the back, which is how Dad takes care of things.

No, Reese would use that knife to cut off little bits of Aiden before he kills him. Reese is even more dangerous when it comes to my safety. Probably because he was the one who found me, starving and filthy, locked in my dead mother's car while her body rotted after she'd OD'd.

I would've been dead in a few hours if Reese and Bryant hadn't discovered me while they were scavenging an abandoned warehouse where suburbanites met their dealers. They'd been hoping to find a few blissed users they could relieve of purses and wallets. At five and seven, Reese and Bryant had been experienced pickers.

They hadn't expected to find a dead addict and her toddler in a locked car in a dark, forgotten corner of the garage. I owe them my life. But I don't owe them every damn second of the rest of my life.

Finally, I have coffee in hand and feel ready to take on my brother. "What are you doing here? Dad said he was going to talk to you and Bryant about getting together tonight. Why are you here now?"

He looks over his shoulder at me, eyebrows curved over pale blue eyes. "So now I need a reason to drop by?"

No, he doesn't. Reese and I are close, possibly closer than any of my other siblings. We're a lot alike. And that usually means trouble for me because he knows me so well he can read my mind.

Sighing, I take a sip of coffee then let my eyes close in bliss. Caffeine. Finally. Reese waits patiently until I open my eyes.

"Now spill it. What happened? Dad's freaked and so's Maylyn. The only reason Bryant's not here is because I told him you'd be more likely to talk to me alone."

"What makes you think that?"

"Because it's true."

I concede the point with an eye roll and take another sip of coffee. Maybe if I ignore him—

"Talk, Olivia. Now."

Walking over to the couch, I sit beside Reese, handing over the coffee because I know he wants a sip. The whole reading of the mind goes both ways. Since I've had more time to think about what happened, I have an answer ready.

"The guy knew I was coming. He was expecting me."

Reese has already talked to my dad so I know he has the information I passed along. But because this is Reese, and I'm dying to talk to someone about what happened, I want to tell him everything. Or almost everything. I just need to do it at my own pace.

"And you still don't know who he is?"

"No, but he told me his name is Aiden."

Reese's eyes narrow. "What do you mean, he told you? When did he *tell* you his name?"

See, this is why Reese is dangerous. He knows me too well. Yeah, and maybe you want him to dig.

"Livvie?" Reese puts my coffee on the table, and I sigh and lean over to grab the mug. "What the hell happened last night?"

"I told you." I avoid looking at him by taking another sip of coffee. "I think he knew I was coming."

"Did he say that?"

I shake my head and force myself to meet his eyes.

"No, but he was waiting for me to leave. He knew what I was there for. He knew how I'd gotten into the house."

"Jesus. Did you miss some piece of his security?"

I shake my head. "I didn't miss anything. I'm good and you know it."

His eyebrows rise. "Maybe you're a little too cocky."

"No. Not about this. There's no way I'd do anything that would hurt Dad."

He grimaces. "I know that." A sigh. "Shit. All right. We need to find out who this guy is, and we need to do it now."

Frustration gnaws at my gut. I rub my hands over my arms, a tell I've tried to eliminate. "I tried. I didn't have as much time as I wanted to do recon, but whoever he is, so far he's a ghost. I couldn't find a match for him anywhere online. I don't know if Aiden is his real name. I don't know if he owns the house or if he's some whack job who's just playing with us. Dad didn't give me much to go on, but nothing I found made me think I was walking into a trap."

Reese's lips flatten, and something in his expression makes my intuition sit up and take notice.

"What exactly did Dad tell you about the information he wanted you to steal?" Reese asks.

"That if he doesn't get the file, Vincenzo will have Dad killed. Dad told me he owes Vincenzo for the Bartram job."

A fucked-up mess from start to finish. And the kind of job Dad doesn't do anymore. Dad told me the less I knew about that, the better. Which I understand. There are things Dad doesn't need to know about me.

Reese knows all my sins and he still loves me. Even though I've done my best sometimes to make him hate me. Thank God Reese is so much smarter than I am.

Reese lets out a sigh as he shakes his head.

"You need to talk to Dad. There's shit he's not telling you and..."

He trails off, and I smack his thigh, trying to get him to continue.

"What? What's he not telling me?"

I know it sounds ridiculous, but I guess I thought Dad wouldn't lie to me. I mean, I know he has secrets, but I never thought he'd put me in danger without giving me all the facts I need to keep safe. I don't think of myself as naïve, but I've always figured if you can't trust your family, who can you trust?

"Come on." Reese stands and holds out his hand to pull me to my feet. "Let's go talk to Dad and see if we can figure out what the actual fuck is going on."

ELEVEN

Aiden

"NO, I'm not going to give approval for that contract until the Saudis pony up another ten million for the construction costs and security measures. We've already sunk as much into that damn deal as we're going to, and if they can't scrape the money together, tell them they're in breach and they need to pay back our costs."

I disconnect the conference call before anyone can continue to plead for more time and piss me off even more. Lately, I've had to handle more of these problems—all related to deals made by my father. For the past two years, I swear that's all I've been doing. Cleaning up his messes. Before Granddad signed over everything to me, he'd let my dad attempt to prove he could handle Squire Incorporated.

That little experiment had been a fucking joke and cost the company hundreds of millions of dollars, money my father laughingly describes as the cost of doing business in today's market. He says I'm too conservative, that we need to take risks to make money. I tell him he's a goddamn idiot who doesn't understand that risks need to be balanced with brains. Of which he has none.

That didn't go over well. I don't give a shit. My father is a reckless bastard who believes he's misunderstood by his father, and his rightful place was usurped by his bastard son, and he takes every opportunity to fuck with me, which only weakens the company.

Of course, he doesn't see that. He only sees the effect my denials have on his reputation.

Too fucking bad.

At thirty-two, I've made more money for the company than my father has at fifty-eight. Hell, my father nearly cost us the entire company in a fucking high-stakes poker game that he tried to win by cheating.

"Idiot" doesn't do him justice. And now this. Another deal he's made on the verge of collapse with no way to recoup what he sank into it. Will this be the final straw on Granddad's back? Will he finally allow me to boot my father to the curb?

I'm not getting my hopes up. For some reason, Granddad gives my father more leeway than he's ever given me. One of these days, I plan to ask him why, though I suspect the answer will be because he knew my father would never be fit to run Squire. And he knew I would be.

Of course, if Granddad does get rid of my father, it'd mean I'd have to step forward or find someone to be the public face of the company. I've tried to get Giselle to consider it, but so far, my sister has refused. According to Granddad, she enjoys her life as a socialite too much, doesn't want to work for the business that provides her with the lifestyle she's grown accustomed to.

Which is bullshit. My younger half-sister is spoiled, but she's not a brat. She does, however, think our grandfather is the devil. It's one of the only things we disagree on.

Standing, I walk to the window overlooking the city. From up here, it's all sharp angles and shadows, with the Schuylkill River sparkling in the distance. I have more calls to make, and I need to make them in the next hour, but I'm still standing there fifteen minutes later when my father storms into my office.

"You managed to screw a hundred-million-dollar deal in a two-minute phone call. What the fuck are you thinking?"

"I'm so sorry, Mr. Knight." Jeannie sounds breathless and pissed off. "He refused to stop."

Turning, I see my father standing on the other side of my desk, righteous indignation written all over his face in angry red. Mark Battle looks ready to have a meltdown, and I have to hide a smile. I don't do things simply to piss off my father, but when it happens, it's a bonus.

Right now, he's livid.

Ignoring him for the moment, I look at Jeannie, who's pissed but otherwise none the worse for wear. If Mark had touched her, I would've had no trouble punching him in the face for daring to. Honestly, I almost wish he had.

"Not your fault, Jeannie. I'll deal with him."

My father hates to be ignored. Probably because his

father has gotten so good at it. Granddad has gotten sick of listening to him. Sick of his excuses, sick of his lies, sick of his smug-ass face. Sick of the way he never takes responsibility for the fuckups but is always quick to take credit for the win, whether it's his or not.

I know that when Jeannie closes the door behind her, he's going to lose his shit. The entertainment never stops with Mark. And I'm not disappointed.

"Do you have any idea what you've just cost this company?" Mark starts in. His voice blasts through the room, as if he has any power to effect change in this situation. "I don't know what the hell you're on, but if you think you're going to destroy this deal just to make me look foolish, be prepared to take a fall this."

I don't interrupt because I know from experience that interrupting him only makes him talk more. If I let him get it all out at once, he doesn't have much left to do but stammer and repeat himself when I cut him back down to size.

"That deal has been in the works for five years and would've made this company a billion dollars. And you tore it apart because of spite. When are you going to grow up, Aiden?"

I wait a few seconds, making sure he's finished, though I know he won't be able to keep his mouth shut once I start.

"That deal was shit from the beginning." I don't raise my voice. I don't need to. "But you knew that and chose to ignore it. It was costing us more than we were ever going to make back. You let your ego and your dick get in the way of business and that's unforgivable. If you'd get your head out of your ass, you'd realize you fucked this deal from the start. You never should've slept with Bernier's wife, because if you'd kept your damn dick in your pants, he wouldn't have been able to pressure you into making this shit deal."

I stare straight at my father the entire time, watching his cheeks flush and his face compress into folds of fury. It's not a good look on him, and I can't quite contain my amusement. My father is a first-class prick and entitled asshole who thinks the world actively works against him. What he doesn't realize is that he brings most of it on himself. I just sit back and watch it all fall apart around him and enjoy the aftermath.

Obviously, there isn't much love lost between us.

"You don't have any idea what you're talking about." He practically spits the words at me, but I'm used to his tactics. "Once again, your information is wrong. If you could pull your head out of the old man's ass long enough to think for yourself, you'd realize the world isn't built solely for his pleasure."

This is an old argument, but I let him rant because, frankly, I enjoy the fact that he's so pissed off but unable to do anything about it. He no longer has any real power in the company. Granddad allows him money to play at being a businessman, but mainly he just makes a mess and I'm always the one who has to clean it up.

I'm pretty sure that pisses him off more than anything else.

I don't understand why Granddad hasn't cut him off yet. Yes, he's his son, but he's my father, and he's never given me anything but grief. I can't remember a time when he wasn't an ass to me. I gave up making excuses for him when my mother dumped me on his doorstep. She wasn't much of a prize either, but at least she'd made an effort before she'd taken what money she could get out of my grandfather and got as far away from us as she could.

I used to wonder what my life would've been like if she'd kept me. Until I got old enough to track her down and realized just how big a bullet I'd dodged. I probably would've ended up a drug addict just like her, living in Los Angeles turning tricks.

I occasionally get a call from her. Sometimes, she needs money, usually for my two younger half-brothers who live with their father. For some reason, they think I'm a decent person. Someday they'll realize I'm not. Until then, I let them keep their illusions and I pay for their school, their clothes, their house, whatever they need. And I keep them far removed from this life.

My father has continued to rant for the past few minutes, but he finally looks like he's winding down again. Time to get rid of him. It shouldn't be that difficult. Usually after one of his tirades, he slinks out of the office and I don't see him until he needs money. Then he slinks back, and we start the process again.

I usually don't get sick of playing. Except today, his tantrum doesn't give me the usual charge. I've got too much real work to accomplish. The real work that keeps the empire my grandfather built churning every day. The empire Patrick Maloney carelessly almost destroyed.

Family can be your greatest strength. Or your greatest weakness.

"—short-sighted and ignorant—"

"Are you finished?"

I've taken my father off guard and his mouth hangs open like a landed fish. I don't usually cut him off like this, but right now, he's bothering the shit out of me.

He blinks and scrambles to find his footing. "No, I'm not. You can't—"

Ah, my bad. I asked a question. "Yes, actually, you are finished. And yes, I can. I can pretty much do anything I want, Dad." I infuse the word with as much sarcasm as I can muster. "And do you know why? Because I'm not an idiot."

Mark blinks, his lips part, and he looks ready to speak again but I've had my fill of him today. I don't want to listen to his shit anymore. I'd much rather listen to paint dry. Or relive last night. I've managed to keep the memories from pushing to the forefront, to keep my head where it needs to be, but now my brain has begun to wander. Now I want to be alone.

As I watch, Mark's back straightens, and he glares at me, a look I learned to ignore twenty years ago. Now, though, it grates.

Everything about him annoys the shit out of me. His voice, his beady eyes, his paunchy body. We look nothing alike, and I'm grateful for that every day.

"I have work to do so—"

"You honestly believe he loves you, don't you?"

My father stares at me with a look I've never seen on

his face before. It's almost like...pity. Which is ridiculous. There are many emotions my father has for me but I'm pretty sure none of them are pity. None of them are love, either.

"I believe it's time for you to leave."

He nods, and his expression clears. "I'm sure you do. And I'm going to. I just have one more thing to say, son." His emphasis on the last word doesn't escape me. "Your grandfather cares for nothing and no one. The only reason he tolerates you is because you're useful. Just be ready for the inevitable backstabbing. Because if you think you're different, that he somehow has feelings for you because he uses you to do his dirty work, then you're just as much a fool as you think I am."

My father turns on his heel and heads for the door. Unlike most of the times he's left this office after a confrontation, he doesn't stomp, doesn't stalk. It's almost like he thinks he won. Which is ridiculous. He never wins. That's the problem.

He doesn't slam the door as he goes, either. Just closes it behind him with a snick.

What the hell angle is the bastard playing at now? He has to have one. My father has an angle for everything. We both learned from the same teacher. The difference between us is that I know how to use the angles to my benefit. Mark Knight never learned that crucial trick.

Probably because he was always too busy spending my grandfather's money like it was water and screwing women like my mother.

Granddad saw the weakness in him and wrote him off. Then he made sure I wasn't as weak.

I'll never let sex make me weak. This thing with Olivia...she's a means to an end.

When I'm done with her, she'll be forgotten; her father will pay for his sins and my granddad's empire will be safe.

But first, I'm going to enjoy the hell out of having her in my bed for as long as I want.

TWELVE

Olivia

"TELL HER. NOW."

Reese stands in front of our dad, arms crossed over his chest, looking like the badass he is. At six-two and a solid two-twenty, he's gone up against gangbangers and syndicate muscle and come out on top. Not many people have beaten my brother in a fair fight. Not many dare try to beat him unfairly either because if you mess with one Maloney, you mess with them all.

And Bryant is every bit as imposing as Reese as he sprawls on the chair across from me in our dad's living room. They're ripped from their chests and arms to their abs and legs. But they're not just muscle-bound thugs. They're some of the smartest guys I know. Both have degrees in business from Temple. They're less than a year apart in age and they took every class together. It took them almost seven years to finish, between working full-time and starting their own garage, but they did it. I've never seen my dad as proud as he was the day they received their diplomas.

Right now, he looks like he wants to strangle them.

Bryant had been here already when Reese and I had arrived and my stomach had begun to work itself into the huge knot it was in now.

"Dad? What's going on?"

With a loud sigh, he meets my gaze. "I know how this is going to sound but...I honestly didn't have a clue what was going on before you showed me that paper." He shakes his head. "Now... I think your brothers are right, so..."

Running a hand through his hair, he leans back in his chair. "Twenty years ago, we were flat broke and squatting in some abandoned apartment building. Your mom and I were trying our damnedest to make ends meet without resorting to...things we didn't want to do. But I wasn't going to let my kids starve. I didn't want you to ever have to live like I did growing up."

Dad doesn't talk a lot about his childhood, probably because it'd sucked. Druggie mom, nonexistent dad. Growing up in a bad neighborhood where, if you weren't a member of a gang or a crime family, you learned to walk a fine line or you ended up dead, caught between opposing gunfire.

Patrick Maloney had found another way. He'd become a thief. And a damn good one.

"A friend of a friend put me in touch with a private investigator," he continues, "one who handled high-profile clients, the kind whose names you don't repeat or you find yourself face down in the river. We needed the money, or I never would've taken the job. It seemed simple enough. B&E, crack the safe, take the files, get out. But the address was Center City. Corporate job. Something I'd never done before."

I frown when he pauses. "So why— Oh. They expected you to get caught."

He nods. "They wanted to test the response, and I was disposable. I realized later the guy who hired me figured if I didn't succeed, he'd have me killed and no one would blink an eye. Just another two-bit criminal getting the justice he deserved."

"But you didn't."

He shakes his head. "I completed the job. Got everything they wanted and got out without so much as a blip on the security system. But before I handed over the information, I made a copy. I knew that job was my ticket to bigger and better and I wanted proof I'd done it."

I glance at my brothers but they're staring at my dad, waiting for him to continue. "So what happened?"

"The guy who hired me turned up dead a few months later. Police said it was an overdose."

"You don't think so."

"No." His expression is grim. "Because a month after that, the security guard on duty the night I pulled the job was shot and killed in an attempted break-in."

"And you thought the deaths were related?"

Dad pulls a grimace. "Not at first. Not until the guy

who set me up with the private investigator ended up dead, too."

Okay, I get the pattern. "So how are you still here?"

My dad runs a hand through his hair again, making it stand on end. "Because I'm pretty sure whoever was cleaning up their mess thought they got their thief when they killed the guy who recommended me. After he turned up dead, we moved to Florida for a while. I knew some guys from high school working in Miami."

Living in Miami does bring up a few memories, mainly of heat and palm trees.

"But when my mom got sick, we moved back. Since no one ever came after me, I figured I was clear and...then your mom got sick."

Dad doesn't talk much about Reese and Bryant's mother and neither do they. I don't remember much about her, though I know it was her decision to keep me when Reese and Bryant brought me home that day. A few years later, she got pneumonia but never went to a doctor because they didn't have the money. When she finally got too sick to function, Dad took her to the emergency room. She never left the hospital.

I have vague memories of her that are more like impressions, and I have a picture of her that I keep by my bed. She's holding me and smiling like she won the lottery. I'm staring at her like I'm in awe. Maybe I was. Like I said, I don't remember much. She died when I was six.

"But you think what's going on now has something to do with what happened back then?"

He nods. "Yeah. That paper the guy gave you, it's a list

of names. That same list of names was in the file I stole twenty years ago."

Unease creeps into my stomach, making me queasy. "All of them?"

"Yeah. That's not coincidence. Twenty years ago, someone went to a hell of a lot of trouble to make sure whoever was involved in that robbery paid with their lives. And now Vincenzo wants me to steal a file with the exact same list of names? Something's not right. Which is why we need to identify this guy from last night. Nothing about this situation is adding up. And the more I think about it, the more I twitch."

My brain races, trying to put pieces together, to find connections.

"You're the smart one in the family, brat." Bryant's deep voice draws my attention, and I find him watching me with a steady gaze. "You think it's related, or is it all just a coincidence?"

Since I'm still alive because of coincidence, and because I don't believe in fate, I have to consider it as a possibility. Not everything is a conspiracy. Most times the simplest answer is the right one. But...

"Did you ever do anything with the information you stole? You said you kept a copy."

Dad grimaces, and my stomach rolls.

"A few years ago, when Maylyn got sick, I sold Vincenzo that file. I figured someone like him would have use for it. I didn't tell him how I got it. I let him think I'd gotten it from someone else. I gave him every-thing I'had, didn't keep a damn thing because if anyone ever caught me with it, they'd figure out I was the one who stole it."

I'm frowning harder now, and my temples are throbbing. "Why would Vincenzo want you to steal something he already has?"

"That's the problem. I don't know. Everything's business with him but he's not usually vindictive. That's why the threat against you kids didn't sit well. That's not his style. And until you showed me that list, I had no idea any of this was related to that other job. But when I saw those names, I knew something was screwy."

"So this has something to do with your past crimes coming back to bite you in the ass." Bryant's drawl grates. "Wouldn't be the first time, would it?"

Dad shakes his head. "No, it wouldn't. But that means someone's using Vincenzo, and to do that, they have to be a lot more powerful."

I look at my brothers. Neither of them are smiling and the knot in my stomach gets a little tighter.

"So you think someone finally traced the original job back to you and now... What? They're using Vincenzo to screw with you? Why haven't they just taken you out like they did everybody else? They obviously know where to find you." I shake my head. "What did you steal to begin with?"

"Lists of names, spreadsheets of numbers. If I had to guess, it was probably a second set of books. I couldn't make heads or tails of it."

"What company? Whose company?"

"I have no idea. As far as I know, it was owned by a

shell corporation. I never found a name associated with it and when I sold that file to Vincenzo, I forgot about the damn thing. Now you come home with information from that file..." Dad shakes his head. "We need to find out who this guy is."

Shit.

Where exactly does Aiden fit into all of this, and why does he have the information my dad is being strong-armed into getting? Aiden has to be involved in some way with the scheme against my dad. That's the only explanation that makes sense. And even though I know that, I still want to know why he wants me to fuck him to get the information.

"Livvie? What's going through your head right now?"

Reese stares at me with that look again, the one that makes me think he can read my mind. If he could, I have no doubt he'd stuff me in a room without windows and lock the door if he knew what I'd agreed to do with Aiden. Who's probably involved in whatever the hell's going on. I need to know. I have to make him tell me. I have a feeling I'm not going to like his answer.

"Honestly?" I stare back at Reese. "I need to sleep. My brain hurts."

"You're not going back there tomorrow, at least not until we know who the hell he is."

I shake my head at Dad's demand. "I can handle myself—"

"Liv—"

"No." I have to be clear about this because if my brothers or my dad find out exactly what's going on with

Aiden, they'll kill him. I can't let them do that. At least not until I figure out what the hell is going on. "Listen, either you trust me or you don't. It's that easy."

"Damn it, Liv, you know I trust you." Dad's frustration bleeds into his voice. "And I'm not questioning your ability. I'm worried about—"

"Dad, take a breath."

Bryant's sharp command cuts through Dad's response like a blade and the resulting silence allows us all to breathe.

"Liv."

Bryant's eyes are a shade darker than Dad's and his gaze is at least five times more intense. But that's Bryant. The dictionary should have a picture of my brother next to the definition of intense. It makes him catnip to a certain kind of woman. Maylyn and I spent most of our childhoods trying to get him to laugh. And most of our teen years exasperated by his overbearing protection.

"We need to know who this guy is." His tone brooks no denial. "Get me everything you have, and I'll find someone to track your ghost. If we don't find him by tomorrow, you don't go back, and we'll find some other way to get what Dad needs to take care of this problem."

Now they're ganging up on me. So I do the only thing I can. I reach into my pocket and pull out the flash drive with all the information I'd been able to find on Aiden and hand it to Bryant.

Then I lie through my teeth.

"Fine. I won't go unless we know who he is."

Reese's gaze burns like lasers into me. He knows I'm

lying but he won't rat me out. Bryant likes to think I'm smarter than I am so, while he's suspicious, he wants to believe me. Dad just looks relieved.

There's no way in hell I'm not going back there tomorrow night, not only because Dad needs that information but also because I'm obsessed. I haven't been able to think about anything other than having more sex with Aiden since I woke this afternoon. Images from last night keep rolling through my head like a movie. And it's a film I want to repeat.

And some part of me knows that when I find out who Aiden really is, everything will change.

THIRTEEN

Aiden

HALF AN HOUR before Olivia is supposed to arrive, my front door opens.

I know who it is because the perimeter alarm notified me someone had turned onto the lane and the security camera revealed my visitor's car.

A car I knew well because I'd bought it.

"Aiden!" My sister manages to draw out my name to six syllables. "Hey, Aiden, where are you?"

I intercept Giselle in the foyer. My sister always manages to put a smile on my face, but tonight... Damn it, I've got to get rid of her.

"Hello, little sister. What's wrong? What do you need?"

Her eye roll is worthy of an Olympic gold medal, but she throws her arms around my neck and hugs me tight. I return the affection before she pulls away and crosses her arms over her chest.

"Why do you always assume something's wrong or that I need something when I come to visit?" She doesn't give me time to answer, just blithely rolls on. "Come out with me tonight. I haven't seen you in forever! And I promise this isn't a ploy to introduce you to someone. Even though you seriously need to get out."

When she finally stops for a breath, I take in the vision that is my twenty-three-year-old sister. We share the same dark eyes and dark hair. But that's where the resemblance ends.

She's five-ten, slim as a runway model, and a carbon copy of her mother, an actual Paris model who managed to get my father to propose. Dressed for a night at the club in black pants and something silver on top that might've been a shirt before someone took a scissors to it, she wears stiletto-heeled pumps that give her an extra four inches of height, bringing her eyes level with mine.

I love the fact she doesn't give a shit that she's going to tower over most other men she might meet tonight.

"Good to see you too, Elle. But I can't go out with you tonight and I could've saved you the trip out here if you'd called."

Her brows rise and she gives me a look I remember well from her childhood. "See, I knew you'd say that, which is why I'm here."

I grin, even though I know she's going to be pissed at me. "Not tonight, brat. I'm busy."

Her long-suffering sigh is overly dramatic but gets her

point across. "You're always working. You know that's not good for you." Her hands move to her hips. "And you're going to hate this, but I'm going to say it anyway. You need to be a little more like Dad and get away from the business more."

Because it's coming from Giselle, I don't get my back up. She's one of three people in the world I allow to talk to me like this. The other two are my brothers.

"I would if I could, but I am busy tonight. I've got a conference call in fifteen minutes." I make a show of looking at my watch, selling the lie. "And someone's got to work so you can have all that play money."

A huff accompanies the eye roll this time. "Oh please. It's not like I'm not going to school and working at the magazine when I'm not in class. I have more than enough money for what I want. But what I really want is to spend time with you."

Her guilt trip pricks at my heart, but I'm grinning by the time she finishes. "I know you're just yanking my chain."

Her pout is adorable. "I know that. But, Aiden, seriously, I love you to pieces and I know you love me, but you've got to get out of this rut. You're going to end up like Granddad, bitter and miserable."

The insult is an old one and usually rolls off my back, but Giselle must see something on my face because she reaches for my arm and squeezes. "And there goes my mouth again. I'm sorry. I know you idolize the man, but even you have to admit I'm right about him. I don't want to see you end up like him. And yes, I know, I'm a bitch.

Please forgive me." Then she smiles again, and all is right in the world. "So? Are you going to come out with me tonight?"

And that's Giselle in a nutshell. So much fire and life and a mouth that doesn't quit.

"Told you, I can't. You'll have more fun without me anyway. And I actually do have a meeting."

She throws her hands in the air and shakes her head. "Ugh! You're so boring. Jesus, Aiden. When was the last time you got laid?" Her eyes widen and she waves her hands in front of her. "Oh please, don't answer that. It was rhetorical. But just think about your answer. Okay?" A huge sigh. "All right, gotta go. I'm meeting Rosalynde in half an hour. Love you."

She hugs me fast then heads for the door but turns before she opens it. "But the next time I ask, you will go out with me."

Then the whirlwind that's my sister slips through my front door and disappears while I stand there, shaking my head. Seconds later, her Fiat Spyder revs and tires squeal as she pulls away. She drives as fast as she talks. Which is good because, Christ, that'd been close.

I look at my watch. Another ten minutes and Olivia will be here.

What would Elle think of Olivia? They're such opposites. Would they hate each other on sight? Not that it matters, because Elle will never meet Olivia. She'll always be a dirty little secret in my closet. One that leaves me hard and aching whenever I think of her.

A low-level charge has been running through my body

all day, like I've got a live wire attached to my skin. I've been hyperaware of everything, easily distracted and irritable. All because of tonight.

Almost everything is going according to plan. And the alterations I made to the original plan are turning out better than I'd hoped. Olivia will be back tonight. I'll have her again. And drive another nail in her father's back every time I make her come.

I check my watch again. I can't help but wonder if she'll back out.

And if she does, what are you going to do about it?

For starters, I'll give Vincenzo the okay to take Maloney out. The bastard deserves to pay for his crimes. That's the whole point of this. If she doesn't show up tonight... I'll be disappointed, but it won't matter. I'll find a way to make sure Patrick Maloney knows I'm responsible for his downfall and that I fucked his daughter.

I want to fuck her again. I crave her like I've never craved anyone. But that doesn't mean a damn thing to my plans. Since I know I'm not going to get any more work done, I head to the kitchen. I want something harder than soda, but I'll wait for her to get here.

A knock on the front door stops me in my tracks. My heart starts to pound, but I force myself to take a breath and open the door.

She stands on the porch and her gaze locks with mine immediately. She looks bored, maybe even a little contemptuous. My lips twitch, trying to smile, but I keep it contained. No need to rile her up already.

"I wasn't sure you'd show."

Her brows rise. "Did I have a choice?"

"Of course you did."

She shrugs, causing her breasts to rise beneath her purple t-shirt. "You and I obviously have a different understanding of coercion."

I appreciate her attempt to get the upper hand early. If she were a pushover, I wouldn't have been anticipating her arrival all day.

"You can leave at any time."

She doesn't answer right away. Instead, she walks by me and into the house as if she owns the place. That confidence makes me want to grab her, push her against the door, and fuck her now. But I know the sex will be better if I deny myself a little while longer.

I want to see her spread out on the bed on the third floor, ropes wound around her wrists and ankles and her naked body on display for my eyes only.

Closing the door, I walk to the center of the foyer and watch her. She's dressed in a plain t-shirt, battered Chuck Taylor sneakers, and worn jeans that cling to every slight curve and make my mouth water. She's obviously not dressed to impress. But I've found that no matter what she's wearing or not wearing, I want her with the same burning desire.

"If I leave, I won't get what I came for, now will I?"

Passing by the door to the formal living room, which I never use, she dismisses it without a second glance. Her fingers trail along the molding on the wall as she pauses at the entrance to the media room. I suck in much-needed air as I watch her fingers stroke the carved wood. I swear I can still feel her fingers stroking along my cock like she'd done Tuesday night.

My cock throbs inside my jeans, pressing against the zipper with intent. But I'm not about to be ruled by my dick. At least, not yet. There'll be enough time for that later. Right now, I'm content to let her explore, let her steady herself.

"You can go in if you want."

With a quick glance over her shoulder at me, she steps into the doorway but doesn't enter. "I wasn't aware this was a social visit. I'm here to complete this deal and that's all."

She's not wrong. And for some reason, that pisses me off. But I swallow a sharp comeback, and when I don't respond, she disappears into the room. I follow until I'm standing in the doorway she just vacated.

Beside the library and my bedroom, the media room gets the most use. I have an extensive film noir library, everything from the fifties to today. Movies look amazing on the theater-quality projection system. My record collection fills an entire wall. Vinyl, of course. Jazz, standards, some classical. Metal and rock. Michael Jackson.

She's staring at the DVDs like she can learn something about me just by looking at the titles. Maybe she can. Doesn't matter. She's here and she's going to give herself to me again tonight. That's all that matters right now.

"I thought you'd like a little time to get acclimated before I take you to bed."

She strolls over to the albums and begins to leaf through the sleeves. "So we're actually going to use a bed tonight. I thought I'd be spreading my legs in your office again."

I had expected her to come out swinging, and I'd told myself I could handle it. But her attempt to piss me off is starting to work. I take a breath before answering.

"If that's what you want, we can go back to the library. I had something else planned."

Her eyes narrow. "You do a lot of planning, don't you?"

It's a rhetorical question, but I can't not respond. "We seem to have a lot in common."

That manages to tear her attention away from the albums. She'd been flipping through the metal section and stops on a Slipknot album, lifting her hand to trace the letters on the cover.

"Maybe we have a few things in common. But I'm not the one blackmailing a woman into having sex."

"But you will do whatever it takes to help your family."

I hear her release her breath on a sigh, and she turns away from the wall to look me in the eyes, hands on her slim hips. "Of course."

"Even if they don't deserve it?"

I can't stop myself from goading her, but she doesn't take the bait. Hell, she doesn't even raise an eyebrow.

"Family is everything."

"Even if they don't deserve your loyalty?"

"I wouldn't be here if they didn't."

"So you say." I let that hang there for a moment before I walk over to stand beside her, pulling the album she'd been looking at out of the stacks. "Is that the only reason you're here?"

Out of the corner of my eye, I see her lips part. I'm ready for her to blast me. I want her to. I fucking love verbally sparring with her. I don't get to do it often because no one talks back to Aiden Knight, CEO of Squire Incorporated.

I'm not arrogant enough to think I know everything. I'm always open to new ideas. But no one can be allowed to get the upper hand. I'm the caretaker of an empire. I can't look weak because there's always someone out there looking to take advantage.

But here, tonight, I'm willing to give Olivia some leeway. Not because I feel any guilt about this situation but because I enjoy having her go at me.

Her lips close and she's silent for a few more seconds. "Of course. What other reason would I have?"

I let that go for the moment as I walk over to the turntable and set All Hope Is Gone to play. Then I press the button to allow the music to filter through the house. I don't crank it, like I normally would with Slipknot, but set it at a low, angry hum.

"Would you like to see the rest of the house?"

I walk toward her, and she has to look up to meet my eyes. Now, her expression shows the first sign of anger.

"This isn't a social call. I'm only here to pay your price for that file."

She's hot when she's angry. "As I said before, you're free to leave."

She rolls her eyes and lust surges through my blood, heating every part of my body.

"So where do you want me tonight?" She looks over

her shoulder. "On the couch? Probably not. Leather stains. Or maybe you just want me to bend over the back of it?"

I admire the hell out of her spine. She's not afraid of me. Or, if she is, she's determined not to show it. I wonder if she's figured out who I am yet. I'm sure she's tried. But the fact that she hasn't thrown the information in my face makes me fairly certain she hasn't.

"I want you on a bed tonight."

Her jaw clenches, and she swallows hard. "Then let's get this over with."

No, that's not how tonight is going to work. I don't want this to be over fast. I want all night. And I'll do whatever it takes to get it. Turning my back on her, I head for the door.

"I'm getting a drink. What would you like?"

I don't look behind, but I know she'll follow. Yes, I hold the cards, but I'm not wrong about the fact that she wants me. I head for the library and I'm pouring whiskey into a second glass when she joins me.

"Better make mine a double." Her voice holds a deliberate drawl. "I have a feeling I'm going to need it."

I squash my smile before I turn to hand her the glass. A single. "You should pace yourself."

She lifts a brow, takes the glass and downs half the liquid in one gulp. I sip at mine, watching her watch me as I swallow, her gaze locking on my throat then slipping down to my chest before sliding past me to the desk. Swallowing hard, she turns away and walks to the door.

"If we're not going to have sex here, I'd rather be somewhere else."

"Would you like to see the rest of the house? Although you probably know your way around as well as I do."

She looks over her shoulder at me and her gaze burns hot for several seconds before heading toward the stairs.

"So we're going to your bedroom?"

"No, not my bedroom."

Her face wrinkles in a frown for several seconds before she realizes what I'm not saying. A little of her haughtiness falls away.

I hold up the whiskey. "I'll bring the bottle."

Her back straightens and that nose lifts into the air again. "Aren't you afraid the alcohol will affect your... performance?" Her gaze drops to my crotch for a long second before coming back up to stare into my eyes with raised brows.

I don't bother to hide my smile, and her shock is evident, which just makes my amusement grow.

"No, I'm not. You speak and I get hard. You roll your eyes at me and I get hard. Hell, you breathe and I get hard. A few ounces or a whole bottle of alcohol isn't going to change that."

She blinks, her lips part, and I can tell she's scrambling for a comeback. She doesn't have one by the time I walk past her and down the hall. I wave a hand at the open doorway across the hall.

"Dining room. Never use it." I continue down the wide hall and push on the swinging door at the end. "Kitchen. Barely use it."

I know she's following. I can sense her presence directly behind me. I head back to the foyer, to the stairs, and head up. She stops at the bottom. I continue. I know she'll follow eventually. If she doesn't... I'll go back, throw her over my shoulder, and carry her.

The stairway is curved so, as I get to the top, I can see that she's taken the first steps. Her expression is a mix of confusion and anger. And lust. I'm not mistaking that. She wants me too. She just doesn't want to admit it.

I wait for her at the top, my own lust building with every step she takes. Watching her walk is an exercise in restraint. Each sinuous movement makes me want to run my hands all over her body. Which I plan to do tonight. All night.

I know she expects me to fuck her and allow her to leave. Maybe she thinks it'll take an hour, maybe two. I don't plan to let her leave until tomorrow morning. And even then, I'm not sure it'll be enough time.

She looks up at that moment and I'm pretty sure she can read my every thought. A flush stains her pale skin but she doesn't look away. And when she reaches the top step, she looks at me with a challenge in her eyes. One I'm more than ready to meet.

When I don't move right away, her brows rise and she lets her gaze travel around the landing, finally landing on the plush carpet beneath our feet.

"Do you want me to drop to my knees and suck you off here?"

The image of her doing just that practically steals my breath. I have to bite my tongue not to take her up on the offer. Unless...

"Is that what you want?"

She doesn't answer right away, and it takes her several seconds to draw her gaze from the floor up my body to stare into my eyes.

"Maybe I just want to get this over with."

But there's no power behind her denial, and her gaze shifts away to stare at the wall before slipping back down to the floor.

As if she's still contemplating my question.

Before I can do anything I'll regret later, I take a step back. The movement startles her into looking up again, and now she does nothing to hide the desire in her eyes.

"Are you sure that's what you want? To get this over with? Do you make a habit of lying to yourself?"

She swallows hard but doesn't drop my gaze. "Maybe I'm not the only one lying to myself."

FOURTEEN

Olivia

HE'S NOT WRONG.

I have been lying to myself, but not about what he thinks. I've admitted to myself that I want him. Getting that file for my dad is not the only reason I'm here. I freely admit, if only to myself, that Aiden fascinates me. He's a puzzle, a challenge, and I love a good challenge. It's why I live the life I do. If I'd wanted an easy life, I'd have gone to college and been a teacher or a librarian.

And I'd be bored out of my skull.

Yes, there's a part of me that acknowledges I'm not normal. Normal people don't become extraordinary thieves. Normal people don't allow strange men to blackmail them into having sex with them.

But I'm pretty sure a normal person wouldn't have

sparked Aiden's desire. Whatever else is going on behind the scenes, he can't deny that he wants me. It's in the heat burning in his eyes and the bulge behind his zipper.

"And what do you think I'm lying to myself about?"

His question makes me want to smile, and I allow the corners of my mouth to turn up slightly as his gaze narrows. I walked through his front door tonight determined to get answers but also because I want him to take me again. And again.

Of course, Aiden doesn't know this, but if I didn't want to be here, I wouldn't be. Now that we have some idea what we're up against, my dad is already working on a way around Vincenzo. I don't have to fuck Aiden for the information, despite what he'd said. There are always other ways.

"Maybe about your reasons for demanding I come back tonight."

He's good. His expression shows no response. "And what do you think those are?"

My brows arch. "Do you really need me to spell it out for you? I thought you were a smart man, Aiden."

He shrugs, looking completely at ease. "I'm curious to hear your thoughts. Indulge me."

"I thought that's what you want me to do in your bed. I didn't know I was expected to do it out of bed, as well."

"I guess when you're here, I expect you to do exactly what I want."

He's definitely a man used to getting what he wants, to having people at his beck and call. That kind of attitude doesn't only come from having money. It comes from having power. And Aiden commands a lot of power. Despite spending every waking second of the past day and a half trying to discover who he is, I am no closer to having that answer. Tonight, I'll get it, no matter what I need to do.

But first, I'll have him. Because if I hold out and push him too far, I might not get laid. And I spent all last night dreaming about just that.

"Maybe you're just a little obsessed with me."

I don't really expect to get a rise out of him so I'm not surprised when his only response is to continue to stare at me.

With a smirk and a shrug, I walk past him and head for the stairs to the third floor. To the room with that massive bed and the ropes. I barely make it to the first step when he wraps his hands around my upper arm, bringing me to a stop. He doesn't exert any pressure. He doesn't have to.

"If I'm obsessed with you, you have so much more to worry about." He leans forward until his lips are right above my ear. "Because I have the means and the will to keep you exactly where I want you."

I realize he wants to frighten me, at least enough to control me. But he doesn't know me well enough if he thinks those words are going to be a deterrent. Like I said before, he is right about me lying to myself. I don't want this to be over soon, no matter what I tell my family or myself.

Letting my gaze sweep up to his, I raise my eyebrows. "Then you don't know me as well as you think."

His fingers clench around my bicep but I don't feel threatened. I'm thrilled that I'm getting a response. This man likes to be in total control but he's not when he's around me. I can work with that.

"I'm a fast learner."

He's bent down to whisper in my ear and the rush of his breath against my skin sends electricity arcing through my body, straight to my clit.

I'd spent most of today thinking about tonight so I'd been in a constant state of arousal. About what he'd do to me, what he'd allow me to do to him. I hadn't had much control Tuesday night, but tonight, I plan to take all that I can.

I am going to make him give up at least some of his rigid control and I will make him like it. He wants me. I know that as fact. And I'm going to give him what he wants. But I'm going to make sure I get what I want as well.

"Are we going to make it to the bedroom or are we going to do it here on the stairs?"

He pulls back just enough to stare into my eyes then deliberately lets his gaze slide to the stairs. "I think I'd rather tie you to the bed."

The image he plants in my head takes my breath away. Me, spread-eagle on the bed, ropes around my hands and ankles, tethered to the four posts. My sex clenches and my lungs contract on a short, sharp gasp.

"You like the sound of that, don't you?" His low voice rubs against my skin.

My cheeks flush with heat but I look him in the eyes.

"Why do you sound surprised? Do you think women aren't allowed to enjoy being bound? Maybe the question you should ask is why do you like it?"

"I know exactly why I like it." His voice drops an octave, and I have a little trouble hearing him. "Seeing you at my mercy makes me hard."

It's fucked up, I know, to feel this way about the man who has the power to destroy my father, my family. And maybe I'm totally delusional, and he's going to screw me and I don't mean in the physical sense. But my gut's telling me something and I've learned to listen to it.

"Then I guess we should continue up to your playroom."

Finally, I see the first hint that I've shoved him just a little off balance. It's there in the tiny crinkles at the corners of his eyes but gone in the next second.

I know I didn't imagine it and now I have hope that I can do it again.

Leaning back, he waves a hand in front of me. "After you."

Game on.

I climb the stairs at my own pace, knowing he's watching me. Maybe he's watching my ass, so I sway a little more. I don't usually try to call attention to myself. It's not good for someone who does what I do to be notice-able. Right now, though, I want his eyes on me. I deliber-ately dressed down tonight. My jeans are worn but fit like a glove. And my t-shirt is tight, cut slim, and the vee in front shows just enough cleavage to be sexy.

Since I know where I'm going, I don't have to wait for him to lead.

The door to the room is open and a dim light shines from somewhere inside. Everything looks different in the light, not as ominous. Or maybe it's just that everything tonight seems so much different than Tuesday.

I don't hesitate when I get to the room. I walk inside and head straight for the bed. It looks perfectly made, like it hasn't been disturbed in days, maybe weeks. I look around but there really isn't anything personal to see. No family photos, no little trinkets. No sex toys.

Turning, I see Aiden leaning against the doorjamb, watching me.

"How often do you use this room?"

He doesn't answer right away, as if he's considering what to say. I don't really expect an answer, but I am curious.

"Not as often as I used to."

Damn, he actually answered. "Why is that?"

"Are you stalling?"

Not really, although maybe I am trying to pry information from him. Any information.

"Are you in that much of a hurry to get me into bed? Or do you just want to fuck me and send me on my way? This is your game, after all. You set the rules. If you want me to shut up, I guess you can just tell me to."

He crosses his arms over his chest, his expression lightening until he almost looks like he might smile. "Would you listen if I did?"

"Do you want me to?"

"What I want you to do is get naked and lie on the bed."

I haven't spent much time with Aiden but I know that tone of voice. He's getting impatient. Good. An impatient man is more likely to reveal secrets. But that's probably wishful thinking on my part, especially with this man.

"Do you want me to take off my clothes or are you going to do it for me?"

A muscle in his jaw starts to tic and I find it sexy as all hell. Up until now, I've been able to keep my libido under control, for the most part. It's starting to get away from me. My mind conjures up images of Aiden naked. The man truly is stunning and I'm not immune.

I'm going to enjoy the hell out of the sex, but I do have ulterior motives, which I'm sure he realizes. I need information. I need to know who he is, and I need to know what his connection is to my father. And if that requires me to get naked and have him tie me to the bed... I suck in air because I'm having a hell of a time breathing right now.

"Come here."

He straightens away from the jamb but doesn't move closer, arms still crossed over that broad chest. My gaze snags on his hair, those messy waves hanging over his shoulders and down his back, and my fingers curl with the urge to sink into it.

I take my time responding, even though my body wants to do whatever he says. I can't give in to temptation. I need to keep as much control as I can.

I raise my brows. "I thought you wanted me on the bed?"

His gaze remains steady. "First I want you to come here."

God, his voice. It makes my thighs quiver.

I close the distance between us with deliberate steps then stand in front of him with my hands in my pockets. I have to tilt my head back because the damn man is tall. But I'm not about to show any weakness and I meet his gaze head-on.

I expect him to tell me to strip. I brace myself to tell him no. But he remains silent, staring into my eyes for several seconds before his gaze slides down my body. My blood heats, making me feel as if I'm being consumed from the inside out. My lungs need more and more air, and I have to part my lips to get enough.

He watches my every move with those dark eyes that fascinate me. They're not black but so very brown, and when I stare into them, I feel like I could get lost in them. But I can't allow that to happen. I need to be on my toes. Which is going to be hard as hell when he puts his hands on me.

"Take your shirt off."

The rasp in his voice makes my sex clench and my lungs seize. But I decided on a strategy before I came here tonight and I need to stick to it.

I shrug, as if it means nothing. "Sure. But I want the file first. Then I'll do whatever you want."

He doesn't seem surprised by my demand. In fact, he must have anticipated me. He deliberately turns to look at a point behind me. When I follow his gaze, I see a plain manila envelope on a bench set against the wall.

The piece of furniture hadn't caught my eye before, but now I notice it's not a bench. It's a table, upholstered in black leather. Iron rings that match the ones on the bed dot the legs and make it clear what it is supposed to be used for. I've never seen anything like it. A piece of furniture created solely for sex.

"Are you a sex addict?"

I don't think I've ever heard a sexier sound in my life than his laughter. It's deep and husky, and it lights up every single one of my nerve endings. My eyes widen, and I snap my lips closed, which makes his grin turn wicked.

"No, I'm not. I just enjoy...certain things."

I can barely breathe. I force air into my lungs. "Like what?"

His expression sharpens, becomes more intense, and my heart pounds against my ribs. "Things I'm not sure you're ready for."

He's treating me like a child and that puts my back up. I'm not inexperienced. But I'm nowhere near his league, either. And I realize how stupid it is to be arguing with myself about how much sex I've had compared to him.

I shrug, determined to put it out of my mind, and walk to the bench. Picking up the file, I leaf through the five pages, though I'm not quite sure what all's supposed to be in it. My dad had given me only a rough idea of what I'd been looking for. The file is more papers like the one he'd already given me, spreadsheets with numbers and symbols.

But... "How do I know these aren't fake?"

"You don't."

Which means I have to trust him. Which I don't. Not

about this. But I do trust him with my body. And if that isn't fucked up, I don't know what is. Our gazes lock and I have to make up my mind. If I walk out now, I have no doubt he'll let me go. But I'll go without the file. But I don't want to go.

Reaching for the hem of my shirt, I pull it up over my head and set it and the file back on the bench. Then I unbutton my jeans and shove them down, toeing off my sneakers at the same time. I stand in front of him in a pair of cotton panties and a plain cotton bra. I need him to know this isn't a booty call. This is business.

And yeah, maybe I need to believe that myself just a little more.

He doesn't take his eyes off me for a second, and when I turn from the bench after setting my jeans on it, I realize he's moving. Not fast but I'm startled because I hadn't heard him coming. It only takes him a few more steps to reach me and I hold my ground until he's barely centimeters away. Now I'm staring at his broad chest, wanting to take a bite out of his pecs.

I have never craved anyone or anything in my life the way I crave him. Why? Is it simply because of the situation? The danger? The fact that he should be the last person I want to fuck? Is it simple chemistry? I don't know this man at all.

And I want to.

I open my mouth to speak but he covers my mouth with his and kisses me. More like devours, like he's been starving for me for weeks and can't get enough now that he has me. His lips force mine open and his tongue invades, tangling with mine, forcing me to respond. He tastes hot and dark and foreign. Enticing. Drugging.

Every one of my muscles threatens to go limp but I know I can't. I can't let him completely dominate me.

I reach for his shoulders as I open my mouth wider and tilt my head to give him more access. His hands wrap around my hips and lift me off my feet and then we're moving. Without thought, I wrap my legs around his waist and move my hands from his shoulders to his hair, winding the strands around my fingers.

His mouth demands my attention, but now his hands move to my ass, squeezing and molding, the heat of his skin burning against mine.

He kisses me like he's trying to consume me and I let him because I want him to. The past two days since I walked out of this house haven't cooled my lust for him. Time has only stoked it.

I came tonight with a couple of purposes but right now, I can only think about one. Getting naked with him.

I feel him lower me to the bed, feel the cool sheets against my back. I moan into his mouth as he crushes me into the mattress, his mouth slanting over mine at a different angle, his lips hard and demanding as he drags my underwear down my legs.

He's still fully dressed, and his jeans rub against my thighs, warm and slightly rough. His t-shirt is butter-soft, but his chest is a solid mass of muscle against my breasts. I rub against him like a cat. My breasts ache, nipples so tight I want him to pinch them, bite them, anything to ease the tension.

But the tension runs all through my body and I know only one thing will make it better. I run my hands down his back to the hem of his shirt, grabbing it and pulling it up. I want it off, want to feel his naked skin against mine. Every other time with him has been rushed, a frenzied act between two people starved for each other.

This time, it doesn't have to be that way.

But Aiden seems to be caught up in the rush. Or maybe he just wants to use me and I'm ascribing too much emotion to a man who holds the key to the plot against my father. As if he's sensed the change in my mood, he pulls away and stares down at me.

His hair falls around my face like a curtain and I want to rub my cheek against it, but his dark gaze holds mine captive.

"Where did you go?"

I shake my head, forcing myself to recite the only reason I'm here. I need answers. Anything else is fantasy and that's dangerous.

"I'm right here."

His gaze narrows slightly. "No, I lost you for a second."

"I didn't know it was a requirement that I participate."

He doesn't like that. I can tell by the way his lips flatten into a straight line. But in the next second, he's already decided how to deal with me.

"It's not." The arrogance of his voice is offset somewhat by the heat in his eyes. "But we both know you want to. So why not let yourself go? I'm the only one who'll know."

"I'll know."

He pauses for several moments before he pushes to his

knees above me. I release his shirt that I'd had bunched in my hands, letting them fall to my sides. My lungs get tighter with each breath, aching with the effort. I have no idea what he's going to do. I'm still so turned on that if he unzips his pants and takes me right now, I'll still get off. Even though I know it's wrong.

He watches me for several long seconds, as if trying to decide how to handle me. Then he reaches behind him and drags his shirt over his head with one hand. My mouth dries as I'm faced with his bare chest.

Jesus, the man is built. Not jacked up like a muscle thug, but toned and tight and—

Oh my god, I'm afraid I'm going to drool. And when his hands drop to his jeans and flick open the button, I suck in my bottom lip and bite down hard so I can't.

"Want to give me a hand?"

My gaze snaps to his. I swear there's a glint of dark humor lurking there. Yes, he's taunting me but... He's not being malicious. The damn man is seducing me. And I want to cry foul.

But I reach for him, grab the zipper tab and pull. I go slow, so there's no chance I'll damage anything...important. The hard thrust of his erection means I have to work a little harder but finally I have it all the way down and his cock pushes out over the waistband of his underwear.

I can't tear my gaze away as he shoves jeans and underwear to his knees, baring the entire shaft to my gaze. He's so hard, when he leans over, it lies almost flat against his abs. I wrap my right hand around him without conscious thought and I stroke him, my grip tight and my motion rough. He doesn't complain. His jaw clenches and his gaze drops to watch as his hands clench into fists at his side.

Rising up on one elbow, I continue my motion, watching his face carefully. I've gained a bit of an advantage, but only because he's allowed me to. And I don't know if that's because he knew I needed some control or if he simply wanted me to put my hands on him.

Either way, it doesn't matter now. I've come too far. I want him, any way I can get him.

I increase my speed, the skin of his thick cock velvet-soft against my palm. I hear his breathing speed up as well and want to steal even more of his control. Pulling my upper body off the bed, I'm close enough to put my mouth on his cock. So I do, enclosing the head between my lips and sucking on him.

He groans out a rough curse then his hands sink into my hair and hold me close. I could lose myself in this, sucking his cock, making him even harder, but he only allows me a couple minutes to curl my tongue around the head then flatten against the shaft as I take him deeper. Then he pulls me away and his mouth is on mine again.

This time, his kiss is a harsh demand, an order to comply.

I give him what he wants, letting my head fall back into his hands. But in the next second, he's lifting me and flipping me onto my knees. I gasp at the sudden reversal, but my ass presses back as his knees urge my thighs wider. A few seconds follow and I know he's covering himself with a condom, which just jacks my lust higher.

Because I know he's going to fuck me soon.

My chest lowers to the bed, giving him more access to my sex. Then he slides the tip of his cock between my pussy lips, and I suck in a breath in advance of his first thrust, knowing I'm going to need it. Because when he finally slides home...

I shudder, pressing my ass back at him as if I can get him deeper. I'm not sure I can. The heat of his thighs burns against my ass and the thickness of his cock stretches me wide. He's holding still at the moment. I know he wants to move. He's waiting for something, but I don't know what.

I wriggle my hips back against him and that must be the sign he wants. Groaning, he begins to move, each thrust pushing me forward so that I have to dig my hands into the mattress to stay put.

One of his hands grips my hip hard while the other slips up my back, flicking open my bra, and landing on my shoulder to pull me back against him each time he thrusts. I lose myself in the motion, in the heat created by our bodies and the ever-increasing desire that threatens to take me down.

But I need something more, something I can't ask for because it would reveal too much. I bite my tongue and turn my face to the side, eyes closed as I try not to give away more than I'm willing.

But Aiden won't let me get away with that.

Wrapping his arm around my waist, he takes us both to our sides, dragging my leg over his thigh and opening me wide, letting him go deeper. His other arm curls around my shoulders, hand splaying over my heart before his other hand slides between my legs. His fingers tweak my clit as his mouth fastens onto the tender part of my neck and he nips at me, causing me to shake.

But I can't move. He's got me wrapped so tightly against him. I can only let him have me and hope to hell there's something left of me for myself when he's done.

FIFTEEN

Aiden

I FEEL her body go slack in my arms and lust mixes with victory.

She's mine. She's giving herself over to me and I'm not letting her go.

Never.

So beautiful.

Still sunk deep inside Olivia, I hold her tight against my chest as she clenches around me.

I want to move so badly I ache from the effort to hold myself in check. I don't want to come yet because there's so much more I want to explore with her tonight. But the way she responds to me makes my inner Neanderthal want to beat his chest.

I know she came here tonight looking for answers. Answers I can't give her without giving away my endgame.

And I'm not ready to do that yet. Because once I do, she'll be gone. I've already deviated from the original plan and now I'm trying to figure out how I can keep her, even though I know that'll be impossible once she finds out who I am and what I've done.

Another pulse of her body around my cock. I thicken even more as I pull out as slowly as I can, centimeter by centimeter. Her sheath tightens around me, as if trying to hold me inside.

Turning her onto her back, I watch as her breathing returns to normal and her lids flutter a few times before opening to reveal those beautiful eyes. My lungs catch and struggle for air. My muscles bunch, ready to thrust back inside her warm channel, but my brain intervenes, reminding me that I don't want to simply fuck her.

I want so damn much more. I want her complete surrender until it's a gnawing ache in my gut. Then I can't deny myself. I slide my knees between her legs and press home again, tilting my hips to gain another half inch of depth. Every motion is tightly controlled, my teeth gritted against the intense sensation that shoots down my shaft and through my body.

Every part of my body wants to fuck her hard and fast, to lose myself in the carnality of her heat and her scent and the way she grasps my cock. But my brain keeps putting on the brakes because I know, if I can draw this out long enough, the reward will be even better.

On my next retreat, I pull out completely and am rewarded by the disappointed sound she makes. Staring down into her eyes, I remove the condom and drop it over the side of the bed. I'll replace it with a new one later.

Now, I lean over her and reach for the rope on the nearest post. Her gaze follows my hand, and she swallows hard but she doesn't flinch away or say no.

As I lean closer, I hear her suck in a sharp breath. My cock throbs, the heat of her body searing the sensitive skin of my shaft.

It would be so easy to move closer to her mouth, to rub the tip of my cock against her lips, and watch her suck me in. I want it, badly. And if the look on her face is any indication, she wants the same.

But if I let her lips wrap around me, let her tongue slide up my shaft, I'll come, and we'll have to start all over again. Not that I'm not planning to take her at least three times tonight, but this first time I want to savor.

So I unwind the rope from the left post and let it fall across the bed. Then I do the same with the other.

"Arms up."

She doesn't respond immediately, but her gaze locks with mine and her teeth sink into her bottom lip. I want to bite that lip myself but if I do, I'll drag my mouth from her lips to her neck to her breasts and I'll keep going until I open her legs and lick her pussy.

And I'll get to that. But first...

Slowly, her arms rise until they rest above her head. The motion makes her breasts pull up as well and now my mouth waters for a taste.

First things first.

I force back the almost overwhelming urge to suck

those nipples into my mouth and lave them with my tongue until she begs me to stop. I've discovered how sensitive she is, how she squirms when I bite her. Makes me harder just thinking about it.

Focusing, I pick up one of the ropes and wind it around her left wrist. Not too tight but not much slack. When her right wrist is done, her arms stretched out, I take a few seconds to simply stare. I haven't yet been able to figure out what it is about her that fascinates me so much I'm willing to jeopardize a plan years in the making.

If it were only her appearance, fucking her once would've been enough. At least, it has been with other women. No, there's something about Olivia that makes me crave her more every time I see her.

How the hell can I work her out of my system?

Maybe you don't.

That voice again, the one I keep trying to ignore. With an effort, I shake it out of my head and narrow my focus. She's staring at me with those gorgeous eyes, but I break contact and move down the bed.

I spread her legs and wrap the silk ropes around her ankles, baring her pussy. I barely stop myself from falling on her and rutting like an animal. That's what I feel like right now. I can only think about fucking her, about the fact that she's given me permission to tie her to my bed and trusts me not to hurt her.

She wouldn't be here if you weren't blackmailing her.

Another thought I don't want to deal with right now. She's here and that's all I care about. The rest we'll deal with later.

Right now...

I kneel between her legs and put my mouth over her, licking the delicate lips between her thighs and tasting her. She moans and her body stiffens. But not in rejection. Her hips press forward, encouraging me to take more.

Every sound she makes fires my blood. I slide one hand beneath her ass to tilt her up, opening her farther. She tastes like heat and desire. I want so much more. My teeth graze her clit, making her jerk beneath me before I swipe my tongue, soothing the tiny hurt.

Heart beating against my ribs, I suck in air and focus every ounce of effort on making her come. I could lick her all night, love how she responds to my touch. With my tongue on her clit, I slide two fingers into her channel, into her heat. She clenches around me, making me groan at the memory of her tightening around my cock.

Just a little while longer. I want to hold out a little longer to see her completely wrecked by her desire for me. The need to have her surrender completely is becoming essential and I work harder, listening to her every sigh, feeling her every motion.

Her thighs are taut, her belly a flat plane as I lift my head from between her legs. I leave my fingers lodged inside her body, twisting and wringing more pleasure from her.

Her lips are parted, and I want to run my tongue over them, between them. But first, I make sure she's holding my gaze before I drop my head to her belly and run my tongue from her navel to just between her breasts.

I look up again and find her watching through slitted

eyes as her chest rises and falls at an ever-increasing pace. Her breasts quiver with each breath and I hold her gaze as I move my mouth to one tight nipple. I lick the pointed tip, the texture butter-soft against my tongue. When I run my tongue around the areole, the flesh pebbles even more.

Releasing her gaze, I focus on sucking her nipple into my mouth and teasing it, making her squirm. Raw animal desire surges and I bite her, hard enough to make her cry out, just short of outright pain.

My cock throbs at the sound and I switch sides, lifting a hand to mold her neglected breast in my palm. Her skin feels like heated satin. I want to rub my cock between her breasts but that's going to have to wait until she's no longer bound. I don't want to push her too far tonight. I'm already planning more nights with her. No need to do everything at once. There'll be time later.

You hope.

Rising above her, hands planted on either side of her head, I stare into her eyes as I settle my knees against her thighs and brush my cock against her mound. The finely trimmed hair teases my sensitive skin, making my cock bob in anticipation.

"Are you okay?"

She wasn't expecting me to speak and surprise makes her eyes widen. She swallows hard before answering.

Her hoarse voice ignites my blood. "Just do it."

"Spell it out for me, Olivia. I need to hear it."

She doesn't answer right away and I don't know why I've given her so much control. She's already agreed to let me have her, has trusted me to tie her to the bed. Her throat convulses as she swallows and her lips flatten before she takes a deep breath.

"Go ahead and fuck me. I want you to. I want to feel you push inside me. Make me come."

Every word out of her mouth nails me right in the balls. I'm already close enough to the edge that I'm afraid if I accidently brush my cock against her skin, I'll come on her stomach. Her words are rough but her tone is breathy and seductive, no hard edges. She's trying not to give in to the same primal forces pushing at me, but she's losing the fight.

She's wrapped her fingers around the slight slack in the rope, drawing her arms tighter. Her legs slide against the sheets as if she's trying to rub them together, to create friction.

Reaching to the side table again, I grab another condom. She never takes her eyes off me. Her gaze follows my hands, and I swear I feel her fingers around mine as I roll the condom down.

Coming up onto my haunches, I put my hands on her inner thighs and squeeze. I can scent her arousal. My gaze falls to her pussy, slick and puffy, my cock ready to burst. I force restraint and lean forward just enough to rub the tip of my cock between those folds.

I don't push deep, just enough to part her lips, enough for the head to disappear inside. Her pussy contracts, trying to draw me deeper as her hips lift to do the same. I let her take me deeper, let her work her hips until I'm lodged inside her. Not far enough. The next move is mine.

Planting my hands just above her shoulders, I flex my

hips and push against her resistance. Swallowing hard, I let my cock throb halfway inside her before drawing back out. The next time, I go farther.

Each thrust tests my endurance, my resistance to her charms. Every retreat makes me grit my teeth against the urge to slam home. Sweat slicks my skin and moisture coats my dick as she circles her hips, slowly enough to be torture. My breath heaves in and out like I've just run a marathon but it's still not enough. I feel like I'm suffocating slowly.

I have no idea what my breaking point is. Maybe it's her expression, a mix of frustration and yearning. Maybe it's the growing pit of desire in my gut. I only know that the next time she arches her hips, I thrust. Hard.

My body comes down over hers, crushing her into the mattress as my hips nail hers with fierce intent. I'm hard as stone everywhere, muscles straining.

My mouth covers hers, demanding a response. She opens immediately, her tongue tangling with mine, demanding more. At this moment, I'm willing to give her whatever she wants...as long as I can continue to fuck her.

With our mouths fused and my hips pumping against hers, I make sure every time I thrust forward, I make contact with her clit. I grind down hard, making her squirm, her hips rising to meet mine.

I kiss her harder, demand more. She gives it but not without cost. Every time I slide back inside the heat of her body, I lose more of the hold on my control until, finally, it's gone completely.

Without that restraint, the orgasm I've been holding back races to the forefront, hammering at me until I thrust as deep as I can get. Grinding against her clit, I feel her moan deep inside and her sex spasms around me, milking me until I can't hold back.

I release all restraints and come, my cock pulsing with heat. Groaning into her mouth, I fall over her, completely covering her with my body until I have to tear my mouth away from hers so I don't suffocate us both.

Her breath rushes against my cheek as mine does against her neck, both of us loud and unable to catch our breath. I'm deadweight over her and I don't want to move. Sooner or later, though, I'll have to because she won't be able to breathe.

And I have so much more planned for tonight.

SIXTEEN

Olivia

I'M SO WRUNG OUT, I can barely move. And that has nothing to do with the ropes around my wrists and ankles.

It has everything to do with the man sprawled on top of me.

Sucking in air, I bury my nose in his neck as I try to calm myself. But every breath is laced with his scent and I soon feel like I'm drowning once again.

Still, I don't move, just let myself drift in that surreal space where nothing makes sense. Like the fact that this man is blackmailing me and I'm enjoying paying his price.

My eyes open and I stare across the room at the window where I'd snuck in only two nights ago.

How the hell had things gotten to this point? And where the hell do we go from here?

Questions I had no answers to. Questions I wasn't sure I wanted Aiden to answer.

A slight movement of my arm and Aiden slides to my side and unwinds the ropes from my arms. I've never been tied up before and I flex my wrists, working out the slight stiffness. Rolling to the side of the bed to remove the condom, Aiden is back a second later to undo my ankles.

"Does anything hurt?"

His tone holds no apology, just a straightforward question.

I circle my wrists and ankles for a few seconds before shaking my head. "No. I'm fine."

With a slight nod of his head, he watches me as I slide back until my head is almost at the headboard. Then I pile a couple of pillows beneath my head and stare at him. The air holds a slight chill and as soon as I think about it, I shiver. A second later, he reaches down to pull the covers over us. Then he piles the remaining pillows behind his head. I wonder if he's about to grab a cigarette. The image makes me smile and now his gaze narrows.

"What's so amusing?"

That voice of his does wild and crazy things to my insides. I haven't figured out why and maybe I don't want to know.

"Do you smoke?"

His brow furrows as he mulls over what I mean and finally his mouth curves in a slight grin. "No. I don't. Sorry to disappoint."

I'm about to say he doesn't, but I bite the words back

because it would sound too much like normal pillow talk. And this situation is in no way normal. My gaze slides away from his and I turn my head to stare at that window on the opposite wall again.

I want to ask what now. But I don't want to leave. Not yet. Especially not without that file. That's my entire reason for being here. And I want to have sex with him again.

"How were you able to make that climb?"

His question makes me turn to face him again. He's staring at me with open curiosity and, despite the circumstances, I want to answer. But I want something in return.

"I'll answer your question if you answer one of mine."

He mulls it over for a split second. "Agreed."

Then he falls silent, waiting.

"I've been climbing since I was a kid. I started with trees, but I nearly busted my head open when I was eight. I fell out of a fifty-foot oak in Fairmount Park, spent a few days in the hospital. I was lucky. The only bone I broke was my right arm and it wasn't bad. My dad took me to the indoor climbing center as soon as I was healed. One of my instructors was a former Army Ranger. He got me into parkour."

"Guess that comes in handy in your line of work."

There's absolutely no inflection in his voice, but my back wants to stiffen anyway. I don't allow it to. I'm not about to let him make me feel guilty about what I do. He has no idea who I really am, what I'm like.

"It does. It was great training. Not many kids are into

that kind of thing, so my teacher was able to spend a lot of time working with me."

"Does he know what you do with that training?"

"Of course not." I shrug like it doesn't matter but he's managed to pick open a sore spot. "Mr. Jim was regulation all the way."

"Was?"

My heart twists a little. "He died last year. Freak accident on a course. He was training a group of disabled vets for a special Spartan race. A rope snapped while he was crossing a stream. He fell, hit his head on a rock and never woke up."

A goddamn tragedy. A thousand people had attended Jim's funeral. I recognized several others who had the same job description I did. Maybe Jim had known what I did, but he'd never mentioned it. And he'd never treated me any differently than any of his other students.

"Sounds like you were close."

"He was a good man. My turn." I speak before he can say anything else, and I feel him tense slightly beside me. But I'm a cat burglar. I'm sneaky by definition. "Why do *you* have the files I need?"

I can tell that isn't the question he'd been expecting. His eyebrows rise slightly and that amazing mouth turns up at the corners. I almost expect him to pat me on the head and say, "Clever girl."

Instead, he leans back against the pillows a little more, his naked body on full display. Unashamed. I'm not a prude but I'm not about to lie here on his bed naked for him to ogle. Of course, if he's going to let it all hang out, I'm not going to look away. Because, holy crap, the man makes me weak in the knees. And, Jesus, I wish I were kidding.

"Don't you want to know who I am?"

"Maybe I already know who you are."

I meet his gaze head on, unblinking. He stares at me like he thinks he can read my mind. Not happening, but he does have very nice eyes. After a few seconds, he takes a breath and releases it on a sigh.

"Because a man in my position is only worth as much as the information he holds."

A frown creases my brow. "What the fuck kind of answer is that?"

"The only kind you're getting right now."

He looks so damn arrogant, my fingers curl into a fist in an attempt not to smack him. "How can you be such an asshole?"

My dad's life is on the line and he's playing games. Which I knew when I came here tonight. So why the hell am I so mad now?

Because you still want him and you still don't have any answers.

He moves so fast, I don't realize I'm beneath him until he's staring down at me, my chest pinned beneath his. I can barely breathe again but it's not because he's lying on me.

"Have you stopped to ask yourself what possible reason I could have for wanting your father to pay for his crimes?" Aiden glares at me although the rest of his expression is perfectly bland. "You're not stupid, Olivia. You, maybe more than your brothers and sister, know what your father's capable of, don't you?"

My eyes widen at the hardness in his voice, a sharp edge I haven't heard from him before. And that's before I register the fact that he knows I have brothers and a sister. My mouth opens to say something, anything, but he beats me to it.

"Maybe you need to ask yourself if your father's worthy of your loyalty."

There's a furious tone in Aiden's voice and, for the first time, I actually wonder if my dad's told me everything he knows about what's going on. In the next second, Aiden is on his feet by the side of the bed.

"I'll leave another payment by the front door. I'll see you Saturday night. We're going out. Wear something decent."

He grabs the file from the bench then walks out the door, leaving me to stare after him with my mouth hanging open. My first instinct is to rip into him, verbally hand him his ass then tell him to go fuck himself and this deal.

Anger pulses through my veins, spreading through my body until I vibrate. I'm not hurt. I can't be hurt by him. Our affair is strictly business. And yet...

No. I shake my head. There is no "and yet."

Sliding out of bed, I realize I'm going to have to walk down two flights of stairs naked. It shouldn't matter. It *doesn't* matter. I'm not ashamed of my body in any way. And if Aiden is watching... Well, let him see what he's not having for the rest of the night.

I make my way down the stairs, taking my own damn time, knowing he's watching from somewhere. I don't expect him to be sitting in the library where I left my clothes.

He has a glass in his hand, but it's empty now. I've noticed he likes good whiskey, which isn't a bad thing. Right now, I want to fill a glass and throw that good whiskey in his face.

Damn it, I can't let him get to me like this.

I look for my clothes and realize he's piled them on the desk. Below a single sheet of paper. My anger is becoming a full-blown fury and it's probably better for his safety if I get the hell out of here before he does something that will make me want to cut off his balls.

Without looking at him, I walk to the desk, set the paper aside, and pull on my panties.

"Want a drink before you go?"

It's on the tip of my tongue to tell him to take a flying fuck, but I bite back the words and grab my bra.

"Blind loyalty will bite you in the ass."

I turn on him before I know I'm going to do it. "What the *fuck* do you know about my family? You don't know shit about my family. And okay, you want me to ask, I'm going to ask. Who the *fuck* are you? What gives you the right to play with my family's lives like you're goddamn God? And why the *fuck* do you want to fuck me anyway?"

I realize after the words are out that I'm still standing in front of him mostly naked. I hadn't gotten my bra on before I turned on him. Right now, I don't fucking care.

"You know what?" I wave a hand through the air. "I'm sick and tired of waiting for you to give me answers in snide comments and cryptic questions. Either tell me what the hell I'm doing here, or I'll find another way to help my dad figure this out."

He doesn't even blink but his gaze burns and his mouth flattens into a straight line, those sensuous lips hard.

"Are you sure you want the answers?"

I roll my eyes. "Yeah, I am. Go ahead. Tell me whatever it is you think my dad's done that's so fucking awful, you want him dead for it."

"I never said I want him dead."

"Semantics." I slash my hand in the air and watch his gaze dip for a brief second to my breasts. Which just pisses me off even more. "Your actions will lead to his death so in my mind, you're just as responsible if anything happens to him as the man who's threatened to kill him."

When he doesn't answer right away, I sneer and huff and turn away to continue to dress. I've got my bra on and am reaching for my shirt when I hear him rise from the chair and walk over to me, stopping only inches away.

I try to ignore him but it's impossible because my body reacts whenever he's anywhere in the vicinity. I want him even though I know I shouldn't. And the fact that he wants me shouldn't make me happy.

Fury and confusion are a combustible mix. And I'm already primed to blow. Just because I don't reach it often doesn't mean I don't have a breaking point. It just means that when I get to it, I can't stop it.

Grabbing the switchblade out of my jeans pocket, I turn and take him down with a move my parkour instructor had taught me when I started getting those looks from the guys in my group. I'm strong but I'm not strong enough to overpower a man with at least fifty pounds of muscle on me. But Jim taught me other ways to take down a man twice my size.

Aiden is flat on his back before he knows what's happening, staring up at me with the first sign of surprise I've seen him show. Followed by a heat I'm familiar with.

The bastard doesn't even have enough sense to be concerned by the small knife I hold at his jugular. It would take a considerable amount of effort for me to pierce his skin with it, and just thinking about it makes me queasy. But Jim also taught me that appearance can be more effective than action.

"Are you really going to stab me?"

I press the blade even closer. "I'm pissed off enough that you don't want me to answer that question right now."

Something in my voice makes him still, his gaze glued to mine. And then the damn man smiles. Not enough to make me want to actually stab him, but enough to make that heat coursing through me pour into my lower body. With my knees on either side of his body and my free hand braced on his chest, my sex is only inches away from his groin.

I have the almost overwhelming urge to grind down on him, rub my pussy against his cock and make him hard. If he isn't already.

Damn him.

"I guess you could just take the file and run, leave me bleeding on the floor. Cut my jugular and an ambulance couldn't get here fast enough to save me." He lifts his chin, baring more of his throat. "Go ahead. You know you want to."

The problem is, I don't want to. And he knows it.

Bastard.

"Maybe I'll just take the file now and be done with it."

He doesn't look concerned. "You could try but other than that one piece of paper, the rest is in the safe now. You have to know I've changed the combination, which means you'd have to crack it again. And as much as I enjoyed watching you the first time, you can't crack the safe and keep the knife on me."

Since he's right, I don't move. I'm still pissed off, but the heat of his body is seeping through my bare skin. My underwear are paper-thin and only an inch or so above his belly button. My nipples have tightened and now ache.

"What the *fuck* do you want?"

My question comes out much more bitter than I antici-pated but his expression doesn't change.

"Right now, I want you to ride me right here on the floor."

I can barely swallow. His voice holds a growl that makes my thighs clench and my panties get wet. I want to lower my hips and grind my pussy against his cock to get some relief.

Jesus, this night is fucked up.

"Maybe I'll just get myself off and leave you high and dry."

His harsh laugh sends shards of need into my gut. "Go ahead, Olivia. I dare you."

Even though I know I'm playing right into his hands, I

ease the knife back an inch. Jesus, what's one more bad decision in a long line of them?

"Tell me your name, your full name, and maybe I'll let you come, too."

He appears to think it over for several seconds, but I can tell he's just as turned on as I am. Dark color flushes his cheeks. I have a second to think maybe he's actually going to be the sane one tonight and tell me to get the hell off him.

Then he glances down at his jeans. "Aiden Knight. Right front pocket."

I have a second to wonder if he's given me his real name before I think, *Jesus, does he have a condom in every pocket?* Right now, I hope he does.

"Take it out. Slowly."

I sit back, my ass settling against his lower abdomen. He has to reach around me to dig into his pocket, his hand brushing against my thigh as he does. I can't help my shiver but I try to minimize the effect. He does it again as he sets the condom on the floor beside us then pointedly glances at the knife in my hand.

I hesitate, more for effect than anything, then reach behind me and lodge the blade in the floor. It's far enough away that he'd have to sit up to reach it but not far enough that I can't easily get to it.

Even though I know I don't need it and he won't go for it. We're both focused on other things right now. Like, how fast I can make him lose his control. I didn't think I could be turned on any more than I was earlier. Now I know he and I have only scratched the surface of this thing between us. Chemistry, hormones, whatever the hell you want to call it.

It's absolutely insane. We know barely anything about each other, but I want him more than any man I've ever met.

Holding his gaze, I let my hands roam over his chest. That perfectly muscled, amazingly mouthwatering chest. My fingers tweak his nipples, already tight and pointed. Just like mine. I wonder if they're as sensitive.

Leaning forward, I put my mouth over one, sucking on the tip before grazing my teeth over it. I hear him suck in air through his gritted teeth as his hands sink into my hair. He holds it back, out of my face, probably so he can see what I'm doing. His abs tighten as he lifts his head. I feel the motion beneath my pussy and moisture floods my channel, seeping into my already sopping-wet panties.

His rough groan echoes through the room and pings against something deep inside me. I move to his neglected nipple for several long moments before licking my way down his belly. He's not hairy but he doesn't manscape. I blow on the hair around his belly button before dipping my tongue into the indent. His abs tighten and become highly defined as he reacts to my seduction.

This is my time and I'm not giving it up easily. He seems to understand that. With my hair wrapped around his fists, he holds steady and doesn't pull, although I can sense that he wants to. I know what he wants and what I want. Luckily, it's the same.

Scooting back until I'm over his thighs, I unzip his jeans. No need to do away with the button. It was undone.

As if he'd known what was coming. He couldn't have. I certainly hadn't. I'd been on my way out the door, pissed off and frustrated.

Now...

Shaking the thought out of my head, I work his jeans over his hips, just far enough to release his cock. He's hard and hot and I put my mouth over the head and suck him deep. His tortured groan makes me want to hear it again. And again. I love the way his cock throbs in my mouth, as if he can barely control himself. As if I have the control.

Keeping one hand on his abdomen, as if I could actually hold him in place, I curl the other around his hip as I drive my mouth up and down his shaft. I'm not gentle and I'm not patient. My teeth graze the shaft as I sink down, my tongue swirling around the head when I pull back up.

The heat of his body makes me feel woozy, almost drunk.

What started as a power play has quickly become something else. I find myself listening for his groans, wanting more of them. I want his hands to pull at my hair, want his hips to thrust as he tries to get deeper.

He's thick and my lips stretch around him, burning a little, but I don't let up. And I definitely don't release him. I want him right on the edge so that when I finally take him inside my pussy, I make him come in seconds.

Because I know as soon as that thick cock lodges inside my channel, I'm going to come.

Yes, I'm that turned on. Every second I have him in my mouth, under my control, pushes me one step closer to the edge. Every second he's not stretching me wide, I'm that much closer to coming.

"Olivia. *Fuck*."

I don't know whether he's begging me for what he wants or if he's just swearing. I don't care. Tearing my mouth away from his cock, I scramble to reposition myself. I don't bother to take off my panties. It would cost me precious seconds I don't want to waste. I'm so close to coming, my pussy is already convulsing.

When I impale myself on his cock, we both cry out. My hands brace on his ribs and I lift my hips, ready to ride him hard. But his hands clasp me around the waist and slam me down, grinding me against his groin.

My clit rubs against the base of his cock, shock and pure sensation shooting up my spine, making me arch. Then I am riding him, my head dropping back and my hair teasing my back as I shimmy and roll against him. I work myself on his cock, every movement shoving me closer to a peak I'm dying for.

I manage to force my eyes open, so I can watch him. His eyes are closed, his expression set in harsh lines as his hips slam against mine in a brutal rhythm. We both know it can't last but I struggle to hold myself back. My bones feel like jelly, my lungs hurt, and my heart pounds against my ribs.

I can't hold out much longer. The next time I push down to meet him, I break, my entire body convulsing in an orgasm so raw and powerful, I'm not sure I don't black out for a second. But I know he's right there with me when he groans out my name.

I can barely breathe, my heart racing so hard I'm afraid it'll never stop. I can't stay upright and find myself coming down to lie against his chest. His arms immediately curl around my body, holding me close.

Turning my head to the side, I see the small square foil wrapper.

I never put the condom on him.

Oh fuck.

SEVENTEEN

Aiden

MY BRAIN'S so damn foggy, I know I'm not thinking straight. I also know there's something important I'm missing.

With Olivia panting against my chest, it's hard to get my brain kick-started. When she put her mouth on me, I swear my neural network short-circuited. Combined with the knife she'd held at my throat and the blow job, I guess I could be forgiven for the momentary lapse—

Condom.

Holy shit.

My eyes fly open and I turn my head to look. There it is. Unopened.

"Olivia—"

"I'm clean. Healthy." She pauses. "And I'm on the pill."

For some reason, that last statement doesn't make me as happy as it should. I'm going to ignore that for now.

"I'm clean as well. I'm sorry. That shouldn't have happened."

I'm not used to saying those words to anyone, but they're appropriate here. The bigger issue, the fact that I got so lost in her that I forgot something I never forget, is more problematic.

"That won't happen again."

"Damn right it won't."

I barely hear her as she disengages and slides to the side, away from me. My arms tighten but I force myself to release her.

"Is there a bathroom?"

I point down the hall. "Second door on the right."

She rolls to her feet with such grace, she should be a dancer instead of a thief and I'm pissed off in a heartbeat. Her fucking father has a lot to answer for.

Snagging her clothes, she stalks out of the room. I sit up, using my t-shirt to clean myself, then pull up my underwear and jeans. Settling into a chair, I wait for her to return but after several minutes, I'm ready to go knock on the door. She emerges a second later, looking like she doesn't have a care in the world. Which makes my jaw clench.

She walks by me to pick up the paper from the desk, looks it over then turns to meet my gaze.

"Who the hell are you? And I want a goddamn straight answer to my question." She tosses the paper on the table like it means nothing to her. "Now. Or I walk and I don't come back."

"What makes you think I care if you come back?"

Her lips flatten into a straight line. "Are you always this much of a dick?"

She has to know the answer to that question is yes. I'm not ashamed by it. The attitude has served me well to this point of my life. "My name is Aiden Knight."

She shows no sign of recognition, not that I expected her to. Picking up the paper, she heads for the door. I shouldn't say another goddamn word but I can't help myself.

"I'm not sure I'm finished with you tonight."

She doesn't stop. "Well, I'm finished with you for tonight."

She's halfway to the door before I catch up. I don't have to do anything more than lay my hand on her arm to get her to stop.

"Saturday night. I'll text you the address to meet me."

She glances down at my hand then gives me a look I can't mistake. She doesn't want me to touch her. Tough shit. I'll touch her whenever and however I want. I've already decided she's mine and I want her for more than just a few nights.

Pulling her arm away from my hold, she doesn't say anything, just continues on her way to the door. Her back ramrod straight, she opens the door, walks through, and closes it behind her. Doesn't slam it, just pulls it shut.

I want to go after her. I'd planned to keep her here all

night, to make sure I got my fill of her. I'm not sure that will ever happen. And that's a problem.

As I stand at the door, I hear her car start and walk to the window. She drives a vintage muscle car, a yellow Mercury Cougar that looks like it's seen better days but whose engine rumbles with perfectly tuned precision. Her brothers' work, I'm sure.

From everything I've learned about them, they're loyal to a fault to family. Mess with one of them and you mess with all of them. That had trickled down from their dad. If it'd been any man other than Patrick Maloney, I might've understood. But they'd given their loyalty to a man who didn't deserve it.

The man who'd killed my grandmother.

No, Maloney hadn't killed her with his bare hands, but he *was* responsible. When he'd stolen this same information twenty years ago, he'd given it to my granddad's competitors, who'd used it to try to ruin my grandfather.

Granddad was no saint and that file had held his sins, sins that made men just like him come after them. A dark night. A deserted road. My grandfather's car forced off the road and into a ditch.

All because of that damn file.

After the accident, I lost the only person in my life who'd ever loved me unconditionally. And my grandfather became a different man. Bitter, harder, meaner. And he'd molded me in his image.

Back in my office, I pick up my phone and make the call.

"Is it done?"

Granddad's hoarse, frail voice reminds me that he's close to ninety years old. He doesn't sleep much anymore and his mind is sometimes addled but, in this, he's clear. He wants Maloney to pay as much as I do.

"Not yet."

"Why?" he demands. "We know he's responsible for your grandmother's death. What are you waiting for?"

I'm waiting until he knows about me and Olivia. I need him to know that I've taken away something of his. Then I'll let Vincenzo take care of the rest.

"The right time. If we rush this, the wrong people will ask questions. We have to let this play out like we discussed. And when he winds up in a ditch, no one will think twice about him. Nothing will come back to bite us in the ass."

Silence from the other end. I know he's not happy but he's not screaming so that's good. At his age, he could stroke out if he overexerts himself. I swear the only reason he's still alive is because Maloney is still breathing. When Maloney goes, so will Granddad. Then I'll be able to put all this shit behind me.

Including Olivia.

"Don't let me down, Aiden. I'm counting on you to handle this. That man needs to pay. You owe me this. You owe your grandmother."

I hear the fervor in his voice, the rising anxiety and the fury. When he gets like this, there's nothing anyone can do to calm him until he gets it all out so I let him go. It's nothing I haven't heard before.

"If that bastard hadn't stolen from me, my Ellen would

still be alive. She loved you more than anything in the world, Aiden. More than your worthless mother or your weak father. Without her, you would've ended up on the street like your mother, an addict. You would've been dead by twenty."

All true, which is why I keep silent.

"She deserves your loyalty. Don't let your dick do your thinking. Get this done. And when I go, everything will be yours."

He doesn't bother to say good-bye. He never does. The phone clicks in my ear and I set it back on the desk. I wait for it to ring, for him to call me back and remind me again of everything I wouldn't have if it weren't for him.

When my grandmother died, I was twelve. My mother had dropped me on my father, who'd dropped me on my grandparents. If my grandmother hadn't taken me in, I would've been shuffled into foster care. I know exactly how much I owe my grandparents. Still, when this business with Maloney is finished, my debt is paid.

But I'm starting to wonder if the price to pay is too high.

EIGHTEEN

Olivia

I'M SHAKING by the time I reach my car, the effort of holding my emotions in check beginning to overwhelm me.

There's absolutely no reason I should be this affected. And yet I can't control my reaction. It makes me want to scream. And break down in fury.

I manage to get the car started and head back out the lane. I have to keep my attention focused. Otherwise, I could end up veering off the road and into the trees. Nothing about tonight went the way it was supposed to. The only good thing to happen was the fact that I got his name. If he was telling me the truth.

Liar, liar, pants on fire.

Christ, I'm reverting to a child. And my pants aren't what's on fire.

I want to bang my head against the steering wheel, but

that won't end well while I'm driving. I can't believe I make it home without wrapping myself around a tree or taking out another car on the road. I manage to hold myself together long enough to park my car in the garage and start the two-block walk back to my apartment.

My heart hasn't stopped racing since I left his home and I'm trying hard not to hyperventilate. It's close to midnight and hopefully my brothers won't be waiting for me because I'm so messed up right now, I might tell them exactly what's been going on. And that would end badly. For everyone.

I'm halfway to my building when I realize there's a car tailing me. I'm not even surprised, not after everything that's happened. And I'm not amused when someone jumps out of the car and runs toward me.

I glance over my shoulder as I start to run. The man chasing me is bigger and stronger, but I'm pissed off and I'm no damsel in distress. My dad and brothers have taught Maylyn and me how to take care of ourselves.

I run because that's the first line of defense. I'm fast but the guy on my tail has long legs and he's motivated. He catches me just a couple of steps from my front door.

I open my mouth to scream, but he claps a hand over my mouth before I can do more than suck in air. And even if I do manage to make a sound, in this neighborhood, I'm not sure anyone would come to my rescue anyway. Except my brothers. They'd be here in a heartbeat...if they knew I was in danger. The way this is going, they won't even know I'm in trouble until they can't find me tomorrow.

Kicking and squirming, I use my nails to scratch at his

skin as he tries to drag me to the car. He barely flinches. Now, I start to struggle in earnest. I can't let him get me in the car. Once he's got me contained, my chances of surviving this go way down.

With one hand over my mouth, he's only able to hold me with his other arm around my upper body, holding my arms against my sides. Which means my legs are free. My heel connects with his right shin, hard, and I hear him grunt. He pauses and my next kick is aimed at his left knee.

"*Sonuvabitch.*"

He curses and his hold slips a little, just enough for me to twist and loosen it even more. I keep struggling, whipping my head back and forth, moving his head far enough for me to get a decent angle to bite his hand.

"*Motherfucker.*"

He pulls his hand away and I suck in air. I've got an opening and I'll be damned if I don't make it count. As he bends down, I ram my head back. *Yes.* I hear the crack of his nose as my skull connects. Pain radiates through my head, but I can't stop now.

Howling with pain, his arm loosens enough for me to get a little leverage. I smash my foot as hard as I can into the same knee I nailed before and now he's in some serious agony. With blood rushing in my ears, I twist and break free. Falling to my knees, I scurry forward until I can get on my feet. Then I'm up and running.

I know I won't have time to get my front door open before he catches up with me so I don't stop. There's a bar two blocks away that's open until two a.m. If I can get there—

Footsteps behind me and the adrenaline rush gives me added speed. I cut into the nearest alley even though I know there's a fence at the end. That fence has been part of my practice runs through the neighborhood for the past two years. I can scale it in seconds. I'm betting on the fact that my would-be kidnapper won't be as fast.

Not stopping to look behind me, I lay on speed and leap for the fence, grabbing at the links several feet off the ground. I dig the toes of my sneakers into the chain-link and pull myself up. My jeans and shirt snag at various spots but I ignore it and climb. The shirt shreds but my jeans slow me down. I yank my leg up, tearing into my skin. Sharp pain makes me cry out but the man is right on my tail.

He reaches for my foot, but he grabs the shoe just as I'm swinging it over the other side.

His triumphant grin turns to fury as I smash my foot into his neck, and he loses his grip. Scrambling over the top, I drop to the other side of the fence. I don't pause to gloat. I run like hell and don't look back.

I don't stop until I'm back at the garage. My hands shake so badly, it takes me three tries to get the key in the ignition. Gunning the engine, I get back on the street and head away from the city.

I don't know where I'm going. I should head to my dad's but that man could follow me and I don't want to lead him to my dad or sister. I could go to my brothers but they'd put me under lockdown.

Obviously, I'm not thinking clearly because my car is already headed back the way I came earlier tonight.

Anger boils in my blood because I can only think of one man who would try something like this. Aiden must have something to do with this. He's not the kind of man to take rejection sitting down, and I'd pretty much slapped him in the face with it tonight.

Half an hour later, I'm back at his place, skidding to a stop in front of his door.

I'm icy calm and anyone who knows me knows this is when I'm most dangerous. Because I've had enough time to get well and truly pissed in the time it took me to drive here.

I barely make it to the front porch when the door opens, and he steps into view. My right hook is less dangerous to him because of our height difference but he doesn't see it coming. He only has time to take a step back, which minimizes the blow but not enough. It still hurts.

"What the *fuck*!"

He raises his hand to rub at his jaw while I cradle my now-throbbing hand to my chest. But he doesn't raise a hand to me.

"I don't know what game you're playing, but if you want to talk to me, don't send your fucking goons to collect me. I'm not easy prey."

His gaze narrows as I stand there, glaring at him. "What the fuck are you talking about because I don't have a goddamn clue?"

"Bullshit. You know exactly what I'm talking about, you bastard. I'm not some stupid socialite you can order around however you want. I'm fucking you because that's what you want in return for your fucking information. Not because I want you but because I have to. Don't send your goddamn hit men after me again. Next time, I won't go easy on them."

I turn to leave but he grabs my arm. My fist is already on its way back to his face, but this time he's ready for me. He blocks my punch and holds my hand away from my target, which was his nose. His grip is tight enough that I can't escape and I'm too far away to kick him. Instead of struggling, I stay still, knowing eventually he'll have to release me and then I'll leave.

I already realize what a huge mistake I've made by returning. I'm too pissed off, too upset, too frightened. And that makes me even angrier. Because I don't want to be frightened. It dredges up memories I can barely remember. More feelings than memories, really. Nightmares I'd had as a teenager after I found out how Reese and Bryant had found me.

"I want you to tell me what the hell happened. Every detail. Now."

His words hold a command that pisses me off. As if he has every right to my response. "Why should I when you already know exactly what happened?"

His mouth flattens. "I don't have the first damn clue what you're talking about. Why the hell are your clothes ripped?"

He sounds pissed. I examine his expression carefully. I don't know if he's telling the truth or not, but he's certainly selling it if he isn't.

"Jesus, you're shaking. Come in and have a drink and tell me what the fuck is going on."

I look down at my hands. My right one throbs with pain. His damn jaw is hard as concrete. But he's right. They're shaking; my fingers look like they're playing a phantom piano. Actually, my entire body's shaking, worse than it had been when I left here an hour ago. I'm not sure I could drive now if I tried.

The angry tone of his voice grates on my already shredded nerves. But the hand he wraps around my upper arm is surprisingly gentle. And when he tugs me closer, I take a step forward. I immediately stop but he tugs again.

I want to go. I want to wind myself around that big, strong body and let him wrap his arms around me and keep me safe.

Shit. *Shit, shit, shit.*

What the fuck have I done?

I take a step back, panic making my skin pebble. "I need to leave."

His brows lower. "No *fucking* way. Get in the goddamn house and tell me what the fuck is going on."

"This was a mistake." I raise one hand as I continue to back away. "My mistake. I have to leave. I can't be here—"

He puts his arms around me without warning and lifts me, holding me against his chest as he strides back through the front door.

I make a token struggle, which dies because I'm shaking too badly. I hold myself as stiffly as I can, even though I want to lay my head on his chest. Which is so totally wrong, it makes me gasp in air, as if I've been punched.

"Christ, don't hyperventilate. Olivia, breathe."

His command snaps through me like an electric shock and I freeze as he makes his way through the house. I'm trying not to notice how solid his chest is against my arm. Or how much heat he radiates. It's mid-June and the night air is warm, but I'm chilled to the bone, probably due to the adrenaline leaching from my system.

A sense of safety creeps in, which is so stupidly ridiculous, I feel like an idiot. But I don't insist he put me down. No, I just let him carry me through the hallway toward the back of the house.

We wind up in the kitchen, where he sets me on a padded chair at a table. I miss the warmth of his body immediately and curl my hands into fists so I don't reach for him. But I can't stop myself from staring into his eyes, so dark, they're mesmerizing. The intensity of his stare should be frightening.

Instead, I'm calm. And that should be terrifying.

"All right, tell me what the hell happened. Every detail."

He leans forward, hands on his knees. He looks ready and able to rip someone's head off and that makes me feel safe. Jesus, it's been a fucked-up night, and I'm back where I shouldn't be. But for some weird reason, I don't want to be anywhere else.

Still, I can't just give him what he wants. It's not in my nature.

"I already told you. Are you going to hold me here against my will?"

"If I have to, yes." His dominance is like a force of nature. "Now talk."

I bite my tongue for several seconds but he doesn't move and he doesn't look away. And the urge to let everything out is strong. And the more I think about it, the more I think I was totally wrong to believe he had anything to do with my attempted kidnapping.

"I was two blocks from my apartment when I noticed a car behind me. A man got out, grabbed me, and tried to drag me into the car. I got away, climbed a fence, which is how my clothes got torn, and drove back here to confront you. End of story."

A muscle in his jaw flexes. I have a hard time drawing my gaze away from it. All those hours over the past two weeks watching him are coming back to bite me in the ass. I was already captivated by the damn man. Now I might be downright obsessed.

Blinking, I drop my gaze, but now I'm staring at his hands. They're clasped together, his elbows propped on his knees as he leans forward slightly. He's had those hands all over my body and I've loved every second of it.

"What did he look like? Can you describe him to me? Identify him?"

If I start stripping, will he take the hint and fuck me? I don't want to think about—

"Olivia." His sharp tone makes my gaze snap back to his. "Can you tell me what the guy looked like?"

"Why do you care?"

"Because while you're mine, no one is allowed to harm you."

My mouth drops open at the blatant dominance in his voice. "Are you fucking insane? I am *so* not yours."

"While I'm fucking you, you're mine. No one's allowed to touch you."

I want to laugh, but he's clearly not kidding. "You are insane. *Seriously*, you are out of your mind. You're *blackmailing* me so you can fuck me. You don't own me."

His expression holds steady. "I've never held you against your will. You're free to leave whenever you want. Maybe you need to ask yourself why you haven't." He pauses, as if to let that sink into my hard head. "Now, tell me what you remember."

My brain spins, like it can't quite grasp what he's saying. Yet some part of me knows the reason I haven't left yet is because, in some twisted way, I want to be here. And if that isn't fucked up enough, I want to crawl onto Aiden's lap and kiss him.

"I'm a damn good thief."

His brows rise but he stays silent, waiting for me to continue.

"I get in and get out and no one ever knows I'm there. I don't take chances." Well, not anymore. I've outgrown my reckless phase. Although, maybe I haven't, after all, because here I am. "How did you know I was here Tuesday night? How do you know my name?"

"You want to play another game of Tit for Tat?" He leans back in the chair, lifting one leg to put an ankle on the opposite knee. "Yes, I knew you were here. I knew you'd been watching the house for the past two weeks."

"How?"

"Tell me what the man who tried to grab you looked like."

I want to scream at him, but I've learned in the short time we've spent together that he's just as stubborn as I am.

"Tall but not as tall as you. Light hair. Short but not buzz-cut. His eyes were light, too, but I couldn't tell if they were blue or gray or green." I thought for a second. "He kind of looked like that actor from *The Walking Dead*, the sheriff, but blond."

Aiden gets a look on his face that I'd be frightened of if I didn't know it wasn't directed at me.

"Do you know who he is?"

He looks like he wants to shake his head and his jaw clenches before he answers. "I'm not sure."

"Bullshit. You want me to tell you the truth? Then nut up and spill your own."

His lips quirk and the hardness in his eyes softens the tiniest bit. It makes him even more handsome, if that's humanly possible. At some point, I'm going to have to figure out how to stop looking at him like he's just another guy and force myself to see him as he truly is—a ruthless bastard who takes what he wants and doesn't give a shit about the consequences.

And I'm going to have to walk away. Get away while I still have enough sense to realize nothing good can come from this attraction between us. I still don't know who he is, not really. I don't even know if the name he gave me is real. And I'm sick of feeling like I've been playing a game I don't know the rules to.

I stand. He's on his feet immediately, towering over me so I have to look up to meet his gaze.

"I'm leaving. I need to talk to my dad. I need to find out what the hell's going on. And I need to get the hell away from you."

"No. If I'm right about who these people are, they'll try for you again. You're safer here."

"I'll be safer with my brothers."

There goes that muscle in his jaw again. It's his only tell that I've been able to identify but so far I haven't needed any others.

"Do you want to put them in danger?"

"My brothers are the meanest badasses in Philly. No one fucks with them and, if they do, they find out how big a mistake they've made pretty quickly."

"But do you really want to put them in danger? And what about Maylyn? You don't want to be anywhere near her, do you? What if she gets caught in the middle of something?"

He's not wrong and that just pisses me off even more than I am already.

"I'm not staying here." The words barely make it through my clenched jaw. "I'll be fine on my own now that I know someone's out there."

"And what if you don't see them coming next time? What if they just aim for your head?"

I cross my arms over my chest, but his gaze stays locked with mine.

"Fine, I'll stay...long enough for you to tell me what the fuck is going on. And I don't just mean parts of the story. I mean the whole damn thing. I want to know what's in that damn file and I want to know why my dad needs it to save his life. And I want to know why you're the wizard behind the damn curtain."

NINETEEN

Aiden

I HADN'T PLANNED on telling her the truth. At least, not all of it.

I still don't. I was saving that to throw in Maloney's face just before the end. I want to be there when he takes the file to Vincenzo so I can see his expression when I tell him exactly what I'd done with his daughter and why. I want him to come after me, to grab a gun and try to shoot me so the shot that takes him out is justified.

A life for a life, right?

But if I'm right, and Granddad has decided to do something to hasten along my plans... I wouldn't put it past him. As a matter of fact, I'm almost a hundred percent positive that Granddad is behind Olivia's attempted kidnapping. I need to confront him, find out what the hell he's done.

But I need to make sure Olivia stays here where she won't be in danger. And that she doesn't talk to her father.

"I told you my name. It's Aiden Knight."

She frowns. "You say that like it's supposed to mean something to me. I don't know who the hell you are except that you know a hell of a lot about my dad and my family."

"I'm a businessman. It's my job to know a lot about everything."

"But what the *fuck* does your business have to do with my family?"

I hear anger in her voice, see frustration in her expression, and know that if I keep pushing, she's going to leave. And short of putting her under lock and key, I won't stop her. I also know that if I play on this building heat between us, it could backfire on me. But right now, I'm willing to take the chance.

I see her realization of what I'm about to do but she's not fast enough. I have my hand wrapped around her nape before she can move, and I'm lifting her to my mouth a split second later.

Her hands slam into my chest but not in fists. And when my lips meet hers, the heat in my gut blazes through my body and blood rushes to my cock. I want to devour her. Instead, I try to seduce her into kissing me back. I gentle the hand at her nape and massage the tight muscles as my lips move over hers, nipping and teasing.

She refuses to respond and her lips remain unmoving below mine. So I kiss her the way I've been dying to since she walked back into my house.

She stops trying to push me away, but her nails bury

themselves in my pecs. I'm wearing a t-shirt so she doesn't hurt me. Hell, she just makes me want more. I wrap my right arm around her shoulders and bring her close. Her arms stiffen but she stops trying to get away.

I allow her to hold me at arms' length but I refuse to let her get any farther away. Then I demand she open to me. I slide my tongue between her lips and tangle with hers, sucking the sweetness and the sass out of her and into my mouth. Her taste makes my head spin and drugs me into wanting so much more.

With my hand at her nape, I tilt her head to deepen the kiss, coaxing a response. She fights the need to give back, but I feel her weakening resolve in the slight tremble of her lips against mine. Her fingers curl, her nails sinking a little deeper, and I know she's mine.

Whatever this is between us, it's potent. And dangerous. And definitely unstable.

Moving my hands to her ribs, I lift her off the floor so I don't have to bend as far. She wraps her legs around my waist without any urging from me and instinct takes over. I'm halfway to the bench in the window alcove before I realize that's where I'm headed. It's wide, padded, and close. Otherwise, her back would be against a wall, and I'd be pounding her into it.

As it is, we almost don't make it. She reaches one hand between us to grab my already aching dick and a massive wave of lust roars through me, threatening to snap the remaining threads of my control.

I was already close to my limit when she told me what happened. I wasn't kidding when I told her no one else was allowed to touch her. She's mine and I won't allow anyone to hurt her. The fact that I'm probably the person who put her in danger just enrages me further.

I kiss her harder, wanting more from her than she probably wants to give. So I'm surprised when she wraps one hand in my hair to hold me steady so she can kiss me. Her mouth now demands and I'm only too willing to give her what she wants. One thing I've learned about Olivia is that if she wants something, she goes after it. And right now, she wants me.

She shoves her hand into my jeans, her fingers curling around my hard shaft. Groaning into her mouth, I stop in front of the window and let her stroke me. Her hand is just as demanding as her mouth and if I let her continue, I'm going to come all over my stomach.

But the sensation is too good for me to give up just yet. Her fingers tighten around my cock until it's almost painful. Which just makes me want her to stroke me harder.

I'm kissing her with even more fury, our bodies slammed together with barely enough room for her to maneuver her hand. Now she grinds her hips closer and the pressure of her hand and her hips makes it imperative for me to get inside her. Soon.

I just need to hold out a little longer.

Turning so my back is to the window, I drop onto the window seat, forcing Olivia to pull her hand out of my pants. In the next second, she yanks away, and I reach for her, practically growling like a dog whose favorite toy is being taken away.

But she's already got her hands on my jeans, tearing open the zipper before reaching for her own. I'm not stupid. I shove my jeans below my hips, baring my cock, which stands straight against my abs, I'm so fucking turned on.

I remember at the last second to grab the condom I'd stashed in my pocket earlier. She doesn't notice because she's shimmying out of her own jeans. My gaze catches on the bloody scratch on her leg and anger mixes with the lust.

Whoever caused that mar on her beautiful skin will pay. And it's going to be a high price.

Then my gaze lifts, and I stare at her mound, the dark hair trimmed. She straightens, and in the next second, my hand lies flat against her stomach, under her t-shirt, my thumb brushing against that silky soft patch.

Watching with laser focus, I slide my hand down until my thumb brushes against her clit. I hear her suck in a sharp gasp, see her hands tighten into fists at her sides and her stomach contract. My free hand grips the soft cotton of her t-shirt and pulls it up so I have an unrestricted view.

I can smell her arousal, and when my thumb finally curls over her clit and presses, she moans. Her hands reach for my shoulders, as if she can't stay on her feet without help. Now I'm determined to make her surrender completely.

Playing with her clit, I focus all my attention on her every move. She's so damn responsive, I merely have to brush the pad of my thumb over the tip of her clit to make her shake. I want her to completely come apart.

For several minutes, I work her clit, my other hand drawing her shirt farther up her body. Pressing my thumb against her clit and holding it there, I look up to find her blinking, her lips parted.

"Take this off and spread your legs farther apart."

She responds immediately, sliding her feet a few more inches away from each other and ripping the shirt over her head. Goddamn, she's the most beautiful woman I've ever seen. Sleek, firm, perfect.

She's close enough that I only have lean forward a few inches to put my mouth on her breasts. I suck one tight nipple into my mouth and rub my tongue along the tip as I continue to torment her clit. Her hands tug at my hair until my scalp burns but I don't want her to release me. I want her totally pliant, and I want her to be coming when I shove my cock into her.

I could suck at her tits all day, feel them plump as I lick and bite. My hand between her legs now slides between her slick folds while my thumb ruthlessly works her clit until she's breathing so hard, she's gasping for air.

Still not enough.

Pulling my mouth away from her breasts, I slide two fingers into her body. She's so wet, it's easy to go deep that first time. I stay high inside, stroking her inner walls until she's rocking her hips, mimicking exactly what I want to do to her.

Her expression makes my cock throb with anticipation. Her gaze burns into mine, as if she's begging for more.

At this moment, I'll give her whatever she wants. Anything she wants. But first, I want her to come.

I circle my thumb on her clit, pulling my fingers out of her tight sheath only to thrust them back in hard. Her eyelids flutter down and she braces her hands on my shoulders, rolling her hips in time to my thrusts. I realize she's close on the next thrust. Her pussy clenches around my fingers and she gasps. Deliberately twisting my fingers, I press inside on the inner wall of her pussy and watch her fall apart.

Her channel clamps down on my fingers then ripples around them, trying to suck them deeper. I corkscrew them again and she moans, leaning closer to me, her forehead resting against mine as she shudders.

Pulling my fingers from her body takes real effort because I want to keep pushing her, need to keep pushing her. Need burns through my blood, clouding my brain to anything that's not Olivia. My other hand still cups her left breast but now I slide it around to her back, urging her forward. Instead of coming closer, she takes a step back. She's breathing heavily, her naked body pure temptation. I want her now. I'm not waiting.

I lean forward, grab her by the hips, and lift her, bringing her over my lap. Her knees settle onto the cushioned bench on either side of my thighs, but her hands land on my shoulders and push me away when I would have brought her closer.

"Condom. Now."

Her voice holds a tone of command that makes my balls tighten. I've never had a woman talk to me like this while she's naked and poised over my dick. I'm more than willing to let her have this because I'm too far gone to care who's in charge right now. All I want is to get inside her and fuck her until we both pass out. It's nothing I've ever wanted to do with another woman and I know it's not healthy. And I don't give a shit.

I obey her command as she watches, her fingers flexing on my shoulders, digging into the muscle with delicate force. I'm too fucking horny to make a show out of it so I rip open the packet and roll it down then grab her hips and bring her down.

My control only goes so far.

She gasps as I enter her, and I freeze, wondering if I've hurt her. Adjusting her body, she sinks onto me with a moan and drapes herself around me like a blanket. And that fast, I'm in control again.

"Come on, Liv. Move."

She sucks in a sharp breath and buries her face in my neck. Her warm breath brushes my skin, causing every hair on my body to stand on end. My cock throbs inside her and I wish like hell I'd thought to take off my shirt. I want to feel her breasts against my chest.

When I finish with her here, I'm taking her to my bed on the second floor and getting completely naked and then I'm going to gorge on her all night. I hadn't thought I'd have her again until Saturday so the rest of tonight will be a bonus. And I'm going to enjoy every fucking minute.

But first, she has to move. I'm ready to rock her on my cock when she shifts her hips forward and then back, creating friction that sears through my blood.

Her languid pace is at odds with her hurried breathing, and I groan at the effort it takes to remain still. Her fingers curl into my hair again and tug. I raise my head and she tilts hers back to stare into my eyes. The balance of power has shifted because, at this moment, I'll do anything she wants.

She doesn't say anything, just holds my gaze as she rises onto her knees, lifting off my shaft, then sliding back down. A connection clicks into place, something I've never felt with another person. Something I can't explain and I'm not sure I want to examine too closely.

And definitely not now.

Not while she's rocking her body along my cock, making me so damn hot I swear I'm going to combust. I wrestle with my control but it's fading fast. Especially when she clenches around my cock as she bottoms out. Her almost leisurely rhythm makes it impossible for me to stay still and I thrust up.

Her gasp and the look of sheer pleasure on her face make me bare my teeth in triumph. All bets are off now.

We're in sync, perfectly in rhythm. Our gazes locked, we move like two pieces of the same machine. We have the same goal...to make the other break first. I'm not sure I can win this battle, not sure I want to.

What I do know I want is more than we have. I want her in my bed because she wants to be there, not because I'm blackmailing her. I want her to be someone she's not. I want her to be mine.

My release hits me like a freight train. A shock to the system that makes me yank her down as I thrust hard into her. Tilting her pelvis forward, she rocks once, twice and I feel her contract around my cock, milking me as she comes.

Seconds later, her body still spasming, she goes limp against me, her body shaking, her breath a hot rush against my chest. Her head is tucked under my chin and my arms wrap around her body, crushing her even closer.

"You're staying here tonight."

She tenses, which is exactly what I didn't want to happen. But she has to know I'm not letting her go home tonight.

"I'm not staying."

Her voice holds no conviction and, for the first time, I hear it waver. This woman who never appears to have a weak bone in her body is now afraid. Delayed reaction to the kidnapping attempt?

I hope to hell she's not afraid of me. She hasn't shown any fear in all the time we've been together. Which hasn't been more than a few hours. I guess it feels like more because of how long I've been watching her. It's been months since the investigator I hired began to send me photos of Maloney and his family. Months since I began to focus almost entirely on her.

Fixate is probably more accurate.

She fascinates me and that's become a problem. It's a weakness and I can't have any, not without jeopardizing everything Granddad has built and is giving to me. When my father dumped me on him, my grandfather taught me that the only things in life worth having are those that are the hardest to come by.

His respect and love were two of the hardest. Keeping Olivia would be another.

Because I'm going to be responsible for her father's

downfall. Hell, if I give Vincenzo the okay, he'll kill Maloney. And if that happens, she'll want to take me down just as hard.

"Let me rephrase." I pull back and reach for her chin, tilting her head back to look at me. "I think you should stay here for tonight. Whoever tried to grab you tonight knows where you live and will probably be waiting for you."

Her gaze is steadier now and she takes her time responding, though she doesn't answer my question.

"Did you hire that man to kidnap me?"

I can answer that honestly. "No."

"But you *are* responsible for the shit situation my dad's in, aren't you?"

Tricky question. "Your father is responsible for his situation."

Now it's awkward, because she's still sitting on my lap, completely naked, my softening cock still inside her body. Without warning, she slides off me, getting to her feet and turning to find her clothes.

"I have no idea why I came here."

I rip off the condom and toss it on the cushion then stand and haul up my pants so if she runs I can catch her. But once she has her clothes on again, she stands in front of me with her hands on her hips, eyes staring directly into mine.

She's not afraid of me and that's the biggest fucking turn-on.

"Don't start lying to yourself now. You know exactly why you're here."

She swallows hard and her gaze narrows. In anger. She's getting good and pissed.

"I'm here because you're *blackmailing* me. I don't know who the hell you are and I don't know why you're doing any of this."

"I had nothing to do with your attempted kidnapping. Are you sure it doesn't have something to do with your father?"

She pauses for several seconds and that quick brain of hers is coming up with answers to questions she hasn't asked. "You're using me. To get to my dad. I want to know why."

I can't tell if she's angry or upset. I don't know if she's just figured out what's going on or if she's fishing for information. I do know it's time to change the rules of the game because the game's been turned completely on its head.

When I don't answer right away, she takes a step backward. And then another. My jaw clenches because I don't want her out of arms' reach but I force myself to stand still.

"Are you really sure you want the answer to that question?"

"Are you telling me I'm right?"

"Do you know your dad as well as you think you do?"

Her gaze never falters. "I know everything there is to know about my dad. He's done what he needed to do to provide for us. He fought to keep the five of us together when it would've been easier to pass us off to someone else. He loves us unconditionally."

"He raised you to be a thief. Your brothers are just as bad."

Her eyebrows rise and she laughs. "You know nothing about me or him if you think that. Who the *fuck* are you? You live in this mansion, in the richest area of Philadelphia, but you don't seem to have a job. You're playing with people's lives like they're expendable, and maybe to you they are, but to me, you're fucking with my life, with my family. You're *fucking* me. And what's worse is I let you."

I hear the anger rising in her voice, hear the fury. She's not wrong, not about any of it. And for the first time since I started down this road, I wonder if I'm wrong. If the revenge I've been chasing for the past ten years is going to be worth it.

Six months ago, Liv had been a pawn. Nothing more. Now she's standing right in front of me, and I have to restrain myself from reaching for her and pulling her back into my body. Kissing her and making her agree to stay for the night.

And if she doesn't agree, well, I know that if I kiss her, I stand a better chance of getting her to change her mind. It's time for her to find out just what kind of monster her father truly is.

And then I should have no problem convincing her to stay with me.

"You father is not the man you think he is."

Her expression turns snide. "And how do you know that?"

"Because he murdered my grandmother."

TWENTY

Olivia

I BLINK and my mouth opens to say...something.

But I close it because I don't know what to say. Except that he's delusional. And he obviously has no idea of the man my dad is. If he did, he'd know that was the biggest bullshit he could have spouted.

The one thing guaranteed to make me want to take off someone's head is to accuse my family of something I know they didn't do. And I know my dad. My dad is not a murderer. That's not who he is.

So for Aiden to accuse him of killing someone, I'm ready to rip his throat out and laugh in his face. Which is confusing the hell out of me because my internal muscles still quiver from the sex we had minutes ago.

This thing between us can only end badly. I know that in my brain but my body is mesmerized by the sex. It can't be anything else. I don't know him. Not really. The hours we've spent together haven't been like any first or second dates I've ever been on. There haven't even been many of those.

Nothing about this situation is normal. Maybe that's why I'm drawn to him. He's mysterious, dominant. An alpha male who knows what he wants and goes after it.

But I should know better. Am I really stupid enough to fall for a man like this? Especially one who blackmailed me into having sex with him? Finally, I shake my head.

"You're wrong. It's not true. Whatever you think you know, it's not true."

Aiden has kept his mouth shut while I stood there staring at him, my mind racing. I see absolute conviction in his eyes. He believes every word he's said.

"He didn't pull the trigger. But the information he stole led directly to her death. In any court of law, he'd be liable."

Now my blood chills because, yes, that's entirely possible.

"Then why didn't you turn him over to the police if you're so sure?"

"Because we take care of things our own way. Your family takes care of each other. I take care of mine."

"So fucking me has been your revenge?" And just that fast, I realize. "No, the revenge will be when you tell my dad you're fucking me. You've been the one pulling Vincenzo's strings. You set this all up."

I'm chilled to the bone at the extent of his plans. And I'm sure I don't know everything yet.

"So why send the goon after me? You already have me on a leash. Why the fuck do you need—"

"I told you. I didn't send him. I don't want you hurt."

Huffing, I sneer at him. "Until I don't do what you want, right? Until I'm not under your thumb anymore."

"You were never the target, Olivia."

"No, I'm just the pawn." Furious hurt eats away at my guts like acid. I'm so pissed off at myself. "Jesus, I'm so fucking stupid. How the hell did I not see this coming?"

"Because you're blind to your father's faults. He raised you to be a thief, brainwashed you—"

"You don't have the first idea of who my dad is." The words are almost a scream. "Or who I am. I became a thief because I get off on the thrill. And because I'm fucking good at it. I get paid damn good money to take back things that were stolen in the first place. Did you know that? Or don't you give a shit? My dad's gone legit. But I'm sure you know that, too, right? No, he wasn't always on the right side of the law, but when you have four children and they're starving, you do what you need to do to feed them."

"You don't need to justify Patrick Maloney to me. I don't care. He's responsible for my grandmother's death and that can't go unpunished."

"What exactly are you accusing him of?"

"The file you tried to steal, he recognized it, didn't he?"

I nod because he already knows the answer to the question. He's still one step ahead of me.

"That file contained information that a competitor used to strike back at my grandfather. Your father stole that information for a man with far fewer morals, and he used that information to try to destroy my grandfather. He sent men after my grandfather. My grandmother was caught in the middle. Their car was run off the road in the middle of the night. My grandfather was paralyzed from the waist down. My grandmother was caught in the wreckage. The gasoline spilled around the car caught fire."

My gaze drops to his hands, and he lifts them, turning them so I can see. "I tried to get her out. I got away with a concussion and third-degree burns. Police got there in minutes. And it still wasn't enough. She lingered for a few weeks and finally she just gave up. She died because someone thought they could take what my grandfather had built."

I don't know what to say or even if I should say anything. His voice is toneless, as if he's reciting someone else's story. But his gaze burns. The urge to comfort him makes my fingers curl at my sides. Compassion and anger batter me. Confusion makes me stupid, apparently. For all I know, he's lying.

But looking into his eyes, I see conviction. Belief. And doubt creeps into my mind.

"I'm sorry, Aiden."

His expression doesn't change at all. "I don't want your pity. I don't need it. What I want is to close the books. Your father is the last piece to fall."

"Your grandfather... He was behind the deaths of the others involved, wasn't he?"

A muscle jumps in his jaw. "My family takes care of its own."

"So does mine. Do you want to know why my dad took

that job? Or do you just want to kill him?" I don't wait for him to respond because I'm not sure I want to hear his answer. "We were barely surviving. My parents were trying to make ends meet but they couldn't. We were squatting in an abandoned building. Dad said he wasn't going to watch his kids starve so he took a job. A job that paid well. The man who hired him never expected him to actually be successful. He thought my dad would die trying, and they'd use his failure to learn more for the next time. But he didn't fail.

"My dad did what he had to do to make sure his kids survived. Your grandmother's death was horrible and cruel and never should've happened. But you're blaming the wrong person. Dad said the file he stole looked like two sets of books. Maybe you need to ask your grandfather why he would have a second set of books."

"There was no second set of books. Your father's lying."

His voice holds absolute conviction. But I've been a thief for a very long time. I've seen more underhanded shit than anyone could possibly imagine.

"For what purpose?" I shake my head and stare straight into Aiden's eyes. "You need to ask your grandfather if it wasn't his greed that killed your grandmother."

TWENTY-ONE

Aiden

"YOU HAVE no idea what you're talking about."

Olivia's steady gaze bores into mine. "Are you really sure about that? Maybe you don't know your grandfather as well as you think you do."

We stare at each other in silence while her words run through my head. I know my grandfather. He's cold and hard but he's not a criminal. He's not a murderer. He never would've put my grandmother in danger. He'd loved her.

Had he?

I know all his secrets. I've made it my business to know. I never wanted to be surprised by anything that could adversely affect the business...

The business is all he cares about.

When my grandmother died, he became ruthless and

heartless, a machine with no compassion and a driving need to accumulate more and more wealth. Or maybe that's how he always was and just didn't need to hide it after her death.

I take another breath.

No, I'm not sure my grandfather isn't behind Olivia's attempted kidnapping. He will do whatever it takes to keep his empire intact. And if that means kidnapping a woman to ensure my compliance, I have no doubt he'd do it.

For the past fifteen years, I've taken every bit of shit he's thrown my way and made it shine. I thought I'd learned all his secrets, thought I'd gained his trust. Thought—

Sonuvabitch.

Olivia's turned the tables on me. I'd expected her to fall apart at my bombshell that her father is responsible for my grandmother's death. I'd wanted to show her how her blind faith in her father has put her in danger.

Now, my mind is racing over her accusations and I'm not sure I'm thinking straight.

Time to retreat.

"Stay here tonight. There are several spare bedrooms." Her eyes widen, and I know she's about to cut me off at the balls for daring to tell her to stay. "Or are you going to run to your brothers for help? I'm sure you've told them what's going on."

Her jaw clenches and she's probably grinding her teeth. I'm ready for her to take a swipe at me verbally. I'm looking forward to it, actually. I've realized I'll take anything I can get from this woman, anything she's willing to give. The sex is a bonus but that's not all I want.

I want more. I just don't know how much more. Or how to get it. Or what it is exactly that I want.

The silence stretches between us and now the tension grows hotter. Heat spreads from low in my gut, makes my balls tighten and my dick harden. Finally, she shakes her head.

"I'm not staying here."

It's on the tip of my tongue to order her upstairs to my bedroom. Or maybe just throw her over my shoulder and take her there myself. I rein in the urge and hold my ground. So does she.

Crossing my arms, I see her gaze drop briefly to my chest before connecting with mine again. She takes another long breath and sinks her teeth into her bottom lip. I want to do that. I want to wrap my arms around her and put my lips over hers and kiss her until she can't breathe, and she can't think straight. And she agrees to whatever I want.

"Do you really think you should go back to your apartment?"

Her head tilts to the left and she continues to stare. "Do you really think I'm going to stay here with you?"

I raise my brows, knowingly goading her. "And yet you're still here."

She rolls her eyes. "Maybe I'm still pissed at you."

I can't help myself. I laugh. "Go right ahead and be

pissed. Then take your beautiful ass upstairs and go to bed."

She rolls her eyes, a deliberate taunt.

"I'm not staying." Then her eyebrows rise. "But I'll take a drink before I leave."

Nodding, I turn and head for the bar in the library. I know she's following. I can feel her behind me, that awareness I've never had with another woman. When I turn to hand her a glass filled with bourbon, I sip at my own and watch her eyes close as she takes a decent slug. I also see her hand shake as she lowers the glass.

Biting my tongue over the urge to order her to take a seat, I decide to lead by example and settle onto the couch then raise an eyebrow at her. She stares down at me for a few seconds before taking the opposite chair. Then she sprawls back like she fucking owns the place and my mouth quirks into another smile.

Silence holds for several seconds before a question I didn't know I had pops into my head.

"How did your mother die?"

Her eyebrows arch, though I don't think she's surprised. "Which one?"

What the hell? "Excuse me?"

She gazes straight into my eyes. "Which mother? My birth mother or Patrick's wife?"

Well, damn. I hadn't known there was a difference. "Both."

She takes another sip before responding. "My birth mother was a junkie. I only know her name because my brothers took her wallet after they found me starving in her locked car. She'd OD'd the day before. I should be dead. My brothers were scavenging in an abandoned lot. When they opened the door to the car, they realized she was dead and would've run if Reese hadn't noticed me. Bryant took her wallet then they brought me back to their mom. I don't remember much about her. My brothers tell me she doted on me. Dad says she felt like she won the lottery the day they brought me home. She died of pneumonia when I was five so I don't remember her."

"And she just kept you? Like a stray puppy?"

"No one ever came looking for me, and Dad told me she'd always wanted a girl. I didn't know he wasn't my biological father until I was fifteen." She shrugged, like it wasn't a big deal. "Anyway, it didn't matter. He's my dad. What about you? What are your parents like?"

She talks about nearly dying as if it had happened to someone else, as if she doesn't understand how lucky she is to be alive and have a family who loves her.

"Absent. My grandparents raised me from the time I was ten. And when my grandmother died, my grandfather became a different person."

It'd taken me years to trust him, especially after my grandmother's death. She'd gained my trust with a constant barrage of unconditional love. And when she'd died, I'd been left with a cold, cutthroat bastard who saw me as clay.

My grandfather had raised me to run Battle Holdings, molded me in his image, and made damn sure I knew that the only reason he was trusting me with his company was because he had no one else. And that if I didn't do exactly what he wanted, I'd be out on the street.

And he'd made damn sure I knew who'd been responsible for my grandmother's death. I shake the thought out of my head. Has he made questionable decisions in the past? Sure. Who hasn't? When you run a business this big, you can't get it right all the time. It's just not possible.

Now, Olivia wants me to doubt what I've believed for years.

"My dad didn't kill your grandmother, Aiden."

Since I don't want to continue that conversation, I ignore her statement. "Stay the night."

She swallows the rest of her drink before answering. "I don't think that'd be healthy for either of us."

My jaw clenches. "Nothing about this relationship is healthy. And I don't care."

Her gaze narrows. "So you consider this a relationship? Relationship implies feelings. Caring. What do you care about? Money? Revenge? Power?" She shakes her head as she sets her glass on the table between us and leans forward, her gaze still locked with mine. "Christ, that sounds like bad soap opera dialogue. And I have no idea why I'm still here talking to you."

"Because you want to be. If I've learned anything about you, Olivia, it's that you don't do anything you don't want to."

"So why would I want to be with you? Nothing about this makes any sense." Frustration creeps into her voice, giving it a hard edge. "I shouldn't want to fuck you and yet I do. I shouldn't let you touch me."

"Then why are you still here?"

She almost looks like she wants to stick out her tongue at me. "Maybe because you're just that good in bed."

Laughter catches me off guard. "Well, damn. Better be careful or you'll make my head swell. And I don't mean the one in my pants."

She rolls her eyes and the corners of her mouth curl up for about two seconds before the slight smile vanishes. "This isn't a joke."

"I never said it was."

"I need to go."

She doesn't move and neither do I, our gazes still locked.

"Do you want another drink before you go?"

"You screw with my head." Her tone has a sharp edge.

"I can say the same."

Her eyes narrow at the growl in my tone.

"Bullshit." That one words whips at me. "You're the one holding all the cards. You're used to snapping your fingers and getting what you want. And if you don't, you manipulate everyone around you until you get it. Is there anyone in your life who tells you no?"

I give her the only answer I can. "You do."

Even her sneer is sexy. "Am I even allowed?"

"I've told you you're free to walk out the door at any time."

Her chin lifts and her expression holds a challenge. "Call off your bulldog. Tell Vincenzo to leave my dad alone, and I'll find whatever information you need to prove I'm right."

Her request isn't a surprise, but her offer of help is. The part of me that wants to keep her tells me to jump on her request, to tie her to me so she won't be able to untangle herself.

"And if you find nothing? What then?"

She shrugs. "We can discuss that later."

"And our current arrangement?"

Her brows rise. "You mean the one where I give you sex in exchange for information to give to Vincenzo so he won't kill my dad? That arrangement?"

I squash a grin, but it's tough. She's got a smart mouth, a sarcastic edge I hadn't expected, and it makes me hard. Hell, she could recite the alphabet, and I'd get hard. That's something she can't ever find out. It's a weakness she could exploit. A weakness I don't know that I want to get rid of.

"Yes, *that* arrangement. I'm not sure I'm ready to give that up."

I think I see relief flash through her eyes. Of course, I could be kidding myself. Whatever, it doesn't matter. I'm not prepared to let her go. Not now.

"Then maybe we could actually, you know, try dating."

There's the sarcasm again and my dick twitches like we haven't just fucked. I don't answer right away. Not because I don't know what to say but because I'm worried I might reveal more than I should.

"And that's something you'd want?"

Her lips quirk up at the corners, making my fingers

twitch to touch her. "At the risk of sounding like a child... I asked you first."

"In all fairness, I don't believe you asked an actual question." I hold up a hand before she can respond. "My answer is yes. Tomorrow night."

We fall silent, our gazes locked. She has the most amazing eyes, the color changeable with her moods. Right now, they're a murky blue-gray. Seconds later, she blinks and looks away, swallowing so hard I can hear her. She's uncomfortable, or maybe shy, which doesn't make any sense considering the sex we've been having.

There's so much I don't know about her. So much I want to know. I want to dig into every corner of her and expose all her secrets. But only for me. I want all those secrets for myself. Jesus, how can everything change in the space of an hour? I'm still trying to figure out where everything fits into my life.

Finally, she meets my eyes again. "I'm going home now."

Of course she says the one thing guaranteed to make my teeth grind. "I wish you'd reconsider."

I'm used to people obeying my every word. That she doesn't is frustrating but it's not surprising. She maintains eye contact as she stands, and I rise to my feet as well so I tower over her. I consider going caveman, throwing her over my shoulder and taking her upstairs.

Instead, I shove my hands in my pockets and watch her gaze fall to my shoulders. I see longing and heat and I'm not above using everything at my disposal to get what I want. If she finds me attractive, I'll use it.

I roll my shoulders, get broad across the chest, and let my own gaze fall to her breasts, small and perfectly formed. I want her naked and spread out on my bed.

Jerking her gaze away, she moves, breaking my single-minded focus, and heads for the door. She passes by me, her shoulder nearly brushing my arm. She's almost at the door when I catch up. Following on her heels, I let her reach the entrance before I grab her arm and spin her around. Her mouth opens on a gasp. I cover it with my own before she can say anything.

Our lips meld as I press her back against the door, my hands gripping her hips and lifting her until out mouths are level and I'm no longer bending over to reach her. Her hands fall on my shoulders, pressing me away for a second before curling into the muscle and anchoring herself to me.

My mouth moves over hers, forcing her lips open when they don't automatically do so and sliding my tongue against hers, demanding a response and taking what I want. She doesn't give in easily and it makes me work that much harder to seduce her.

She tastes like sex and desire and I have to stop myself from dragging her clothes off her body and fucking her against the door. Then she grinds her mound against my erection, making me groan at the pressure and the fact that she's so close and it would only take one hand to rip her clothes away so I could get inside her.

And she doesn't seem to want to let me go. One of her hands wraps in my hair and tugs until my scalp tingles. Her other hand wraps around my neck to hold me at her mouth. With her legs wrapped around my waist, she rocks against me, making my cock harder and my blood pound hot in my veins. Every cell in my body wants her. I don't know why I shouldn't have her.

I'm ready to shove one hand down the front of her jeans when she drags her mouth away. Instead of letting her go, I press my mouth harder against hers until her head comes up against the door. I tilt my head so I can slant my mouth over hers and deepen the kiss, my tongue tangling with hers, coaxing more from her. She's holding back and I can sense it.

I want everything and I want it given freely.

She gives me more but she won't let me dominate her completely. She yanks hard on my hair but when I give in and let my hand slid into her jeans, her grip eases and she groans. The heat of her body sears my palm as it slides beneath her underwear and over her mound. The brush of hair against my skin makes my cock throb.

And when she tilts her pelvis forward, my fingers slide between her legs to the slippery folds of her sex. Jesus, she's soft and wet and so fucking tempting. I want to sink inside her and fuck her against the fall. I want to strip off her pants, pull out my cock and sink deep inside her. Just the thought makes my heart kick into another gear.

My lungs are starving for air but I don't want to give up her mouth. Her hand tightens in my hair but now she's pulling me closer. Her mouth moves under mine, just as hungry as I am. Tilting her head to the side, she gives me a better angle and I kiss her deeper, take more.

Which only makes me want more. I slide one finger along her clit and drink in her moan. I play with the hard little knot until she's panting and I know if I push her, she'll give me what I want.

And I want it. I want everything she'll give me. I just don't want her to give me her body because she's horny. I want more.

Reluctantly, I ease back and, when I release her mouth, we're both breathing so hard that's all I hear. Pulling back far enough to look into her eyes, I find her staring back into mine, her gaze is hazy with lust but when she blinks, determination returns.

"I need to leave."

"No, you don't."

Her lips part to protest, and I steal the opportunity to kiss her again. It only takes a second for her to respond, but in the next moment, she pushes away. I reluctantly pull my hand free and lower her feet to the floor.

"Text me to let me know you got home safely."

Her eyes widen in surprise before her mouth curves in a sweetly bemused smile. "Are you serious?"

I stare at her until she shakes her head and releases a short, amused huff before she shrugs.

"Okay. If I remember."

I take a step back and she turns to open the door. I can't help myself. I swat her on the ass, and she turns with a startled expression.

"Make sure you do."

Her gaze narrows, and I wonder if she's about to tell me to go fuck myself. I wouldn't put it past her and I wouldn't blame her. Instead, she dips her chin briefly before she slips out the door. Moving to the window, I watch her head to her car. She doesn't hurry, but she doesn't take her time. She walks with grace and purpose and a sexy wiggle of her ass that makes my mouth water and my heart race.

Some of that is because I'm so fucking in lust with her. The rest is because I'm worried about her. The men who tried to take her are still out there.

But I have an idea how to call off that danger.

TWENTY-TWO

Olivia

AS I DRIVE BACK to my apartment, I try to keep my attention focused on the road, to make sure no one is following me. But I can't keep thoughts of Aiden from intruding. Every kiss, every caress... It all plays through my head on repeat, making it impossible to forget him.

Everything about him is a contradiction. He's blackmailing me and yet he seems to be worried about me. I can't decide if he's just that good of a liar or if he truly cares.

And if he does care, should it matter?

That question doesn't have an answer. And by the time I reach the parking garage for the second time that night, I'm more confused than I was before. I do know one thing. I'm going to clear my dad's name. Aiden's wrong about my dad. I have no doubt of that. But I'm going to need help.

Checking the time, I see it's almost one a.m. I guess recruiting my brothers is going to have to wait until tomorrow morning. I'm super careful when I park, leaving the garage by the rarely used back door, making sure there's no one in the area and no cars moving anywhere.

I take the back door into my apartment building and double-check the locks and the few safety measures I have in place. So when I turn on the light and see someone sitting on my couch, I gasp out a short scream before I realize it's Reese.

"Jesus Christ! Goddammit, Reese." I throw my keys at him, which he grabs out of the air with ease. "What the fuck is up with you? You have to knock this shit off. Don't you have your own damn apartment to skulk around in?"

Reese's gaze locks on to me with laser precision. "Where have you been?"

I don't bother to answer. Heading for the kitchen, I grab a beer out of the fridge then sigh and grab one for Reese. I toss that at him, too, pissed that he easily snags it and it doesn't hit him on the head.

"I didn't know I had to keep you up to date on all of my activities. Last time I checked I was still twenty-five."

"Where were you, Liv?"

My gaze narrows at the rough tone of his voice and it takes me a second to realize he's not angry. He's scared.

Shit.

"I was at a friend's." I shrug, but I know he's not going to give up. He knows something.

He remains quiet for another few seconds before he

sucks in air. "Did someone try to snatch you off the street earlier tonight?"

Well, that had gotten around fast. I should have realized someone somewhere had seen something and had reported back to my brothers. At least it was Reese sitting here and not my dad. Although if Reese had heard, my dad probably wasn't far behind.

"Yes." I hold up one hand before he can continue. "But they didn't catch me, and I'm pretty sure I broke the guy's knee. I got away, no worse for wear. Just like you taught me."

His gaze runs over me from top to bottom and back again. And his fear mixes with anger and makes me roll my eyes.

"Reese, seriously, I'm fine."

"Then where the *fuck* have you been for the past three hours?"

I refrain from pointing out that it hasn't exactly been three hours, more like two and a half. Instead, I sit on the chair opposite Reese and meet his gaze head on.

"At a friend's house."

"I want a name, little sister, because if it's who I think it is, we are going to have a serious problem."

My back stiffens, and I sit up a little straighter. "Reese, you're my brother, and I love you dearly, but if you think you can stick your nose in my business—"

"Where. Were. You?"

"None. Of. Your. Business."

Impasse.

We may not share DNA but Reese and I are identically stubborn to the core. We don't give an inch when we're cornered. But he's also my brother and I love him and the rest of my family more than anyone else in the world.

"Shit." I make a face at him. "You're a pain in my ass, you know that, right?"

He grimaces as well. "I know. I also know you're hiding something and that scares the fucking shit out of me. We didn't used to have secrets from each other. What the hell happened?"

My nose wrinkles. "I became a woman with a sex life, and you couldn't handle it."

Reese's grimace turns painful. "Touché."

Shaking my head, I sigh. "Look, I didn't want to alarm anyone this late, okay? I got away. I'm fine. And we can talk about it tomorrow when we've all had some sleep."

"Does this have something to do with Dad's problem?"

Since it's pointless to lie, I nod and decide to give him a small piece of what I know. Nothing about Aiden, but maybe Reese will see holes in my logic about the other pieces of the puzzle.

"I think there's someone else behind the scenes pulling Vincenzo's strings. And I think it might have something to do with the death of a woman shortly after Dad pulled that job twenty years ago."

Reese leans back into his chair and nods. "Tell me. All of it."

I lay out everything Aiden told me about his grandparents, about his grandmother's death and his grandfather's need for revenge.

"So Aiden Knight's grandfather had everyone involved in his wife's death killed and now his grandson is finishing the job by getting Vincenzo to kill Dad?" Reese shakes his head. "Sounds like the plot to a bad movie. But I guess if you don't want to get your hands dirty, you have someone else do the dirty work for you. I guess this asshole Aiden has a weak stomach. Or he's just a pussy who's too afraid to come after us himself."

Hearing Reese talk about Aiden like this makes me cringe. But he's not wrong. My heart pounds a hundred miles an hour and I'm having a hard time seeing Aiden as the absolute bad guy.

"I'm not excusing his actions, but Aiden did lose his grandmother in a car crash that could have killed him too."

Reese's eyes widen. "Are you actually defending the guy?"

"No, not at all. I'm just... I don't know, Reese. Not everything's black and white."

"No, it's not. But you don't go after a man's kids. That's bullshit. And if Dad's right, he's not the one this Knight guy should be pissed off at. It's whoever tried to run them off the road that night."

"And what if Aiden's grandfather wants to tie up loose ends? What if he's using Aiden to clean up what's left of his mess?"

Shaking his head, Reese leans forward. "It doesn't matter. We need to cut Knight off at the knees before he manages to get Dad killed. We need to take him out."

I knew Reese would say that. And I know I can't say anything else without alerting Reese to the fact that something is going on with me and Aiden. Still, I couldn't keep my mouth shut.

"Let me talk to Aiden again before we do anything."

"What do you mean, talk to Aiden *again*? When did you talk to him the last time? I thought you weren't going back until we had more information. Who the fuck is this guy? And why the hell are you on a first-name basis with him?"

When I don't answer right away, Reese's gaze narrows.

"Livvie?"

I take a deep breath. "Don't freak."

Now Reese's eyes widen, and I'm pretty sure he's gone pale under his tan. "Oh, Jesus Christ. What the hell did you get yourself into?"

I've been dying to talk to someone about what's been happening the past few days. So much has happened in such a short time that my brain is spinning. It would help to be able to hash it out with someone I trust. The problem is, Maylyn's too young, and Bryant would take the shotgun he keeps in the shop for protection and blow a hole through Aiden, probably somewhere south of his belt buckle.

That leaves Reese, who might actually hear me out... before taking a baseball bat to Aiden's head.

Damn it, this is a bad idea. A really freaking bad idea that I now have to talk my way out of. Somehow.

"I made a deal with Aiden for the information. That first night. He knew I was coming. I don't know how, but he knew. We talked," we fucked, but my brother doesn't need to know that, "and we agreed that I'd return for more pieces of the file."

Reese's expression promises pain for Aiden. "And what the fuck does he get in exchange?"

My body, which I have no problem giving him. "Revenge. He wants Dad to suffer so he planned to use me to make that happen."

"I'm going to fucking kill—"

"Nothing's happened." Reese is going to be so pissed if he ever finds out I'm lying. He *will* kill Aiden. "He hasn't hurt me, he hasn't ever threatened me."

"Then what the fuck is his deal?"

"He wants someone to pay for his grandmother's death, and he thinks Dad's responsible but..."

"But what?"

With Reese's attention successfully diverted, I breathe a sigh of relief. "I'm pretty sure it's his grandfather's fault, and he's been using Aiden's grief to cover his guilt. If we can find proof that Reese's grandfather is responsible for the accident that killed his grandmother, Aiden will drop the attack on Dad."

"And you talked to Aiden about this?"

I nod.

"Without knowing who his grandfather is or what the actual *fuck* is going on?"

Okay, now he's just pissing me off. I cross my arms over my chest and stare back at Reese, reminding myself that I love him dearly and that he only wants me to be safe.

"I want you to remind yourself that I'm twenty-five

years old and have been living on my own for the past five years. I'm not a child so don't treat me like one."

Reese has the good sense to look remorseful...for about two seconds.

"You're playing a dangerous game without knowing all the facts. Jesus, Liv, this guy could decide he's going to punish Dad by hurting you." Running a hand through his hair, Reese leans forward, his gaze intent on mine. "Look, Bryant and I have been going through the information you gave us and we're pretty sure we know who this guy is. And he's no one you want to be involved with."

My mouth drops open for a split second in shock. "What the hell? When were you going to tell me?"

"Tomorrow...well, this morning. If he is who we think, you're out of your league, little sister, and you need to get the fuck away from him. What you just told me about his grandmother lines up with information about a company called Battle Holdings. Multinational. Multibillion-dollar assets. We're talking major power player all over the world. They've got their fingers in everything, some of it illegal. If this is the same guy, then his grandfather is the one who had those other guys killed after Dad stole that file. Aiden's using you to get to Dad. Hell, you even know that, and you still went *back*?"

"I told you, I think we can get Aiden to get his grandfather to back off Dad. We just need to show Aiden we're right about what happened. That means if Dad's right and there's another set of books, we need them to show to Aiden. Once he has those, Dad will be safe."

Reese pauses and I know he's looking over all the

angles. My brother may be an occasional hothead but he can also be frustratingly thorough.

Finally, he leans back in his chair. "So where do you think this second set of books is?"

"I think his grandfather has it. And if you know where he lives, I can steal it."

Reese's eyebrows slam down. "Are you out of your mind? There's no way in hell you're going anywhere near that."

I bite my tongue for several seconds before I say something to Reese I'll regret. "I can get Aiden to tell me where to find the file."

"And have him tip off his grandfather? No fucking way. He'll come after you again."

"And I told you, I am perfectly capable of taking care of myself. I'm not stupid and I'm not careless. I want you to give me three days before you go to Dad with any of this. If I can't find what we need in two days, I'll come clean. I'll tell Dad all of it and we'll figure out how to deal with Aiden and his grandfather." How I can do that without telling them about my relationship with Aiden is a mystery but I'll deal with that later. "Three days, Reese. That's all."

"You're really sure you'll be able to find something to clear Dad in that short amount of time?"

I nod. "Yeah, I really am." I have to. Failure is not an option.

Reese is silent for so long I'm almost ready to prod him. "Three days, Liv. After that, I can't guarantee Bryant and I won't start bashing heads."

TWENTY-THREE

Aiden

THE NEXT MORNING, I'm sitting at the desk in my office, forcing myself to concentrate. I've already snapped at Jeannie, who quietly placed the files I'd asked for on my desk, turned, and left the building.

I waited five minutes, texted a sincere apology, and was told she'd return after lunch. And did she want me to pick up anything. I don't deserve her, and she doesn't deserve to deal with me today. I told her to work from home the rest of the day because I'm a prick, and I'd see her tomorrow. Least I could do to make up for ripping into her for no reason. Well, I have a reason for being an utter ass but it has nothing to do with her.

Olivia never called last night.

I barely got any sleep, between talking myself out of driving to her apartment to make sure she got there safely and replaying what she'd told me about the files her father stole twenty years ago. Realistically, I know she's fine. Hell, she probably went straight to her brothers, who would take care of any threat against her. The problem with that is, I want to be the one she runs to.

Which presents a whole other set of problems that I'm not ready to deal with. At least, not yet.

With an angry sigh, I force my attention back to the spreadsheet of numbers dealing with a new acquisition my father wants to make in Mexico, and which I'm pretty sure we're going to pass on, when my cell phone vibrates on my desk.

I check the number before grabbing it.

"I assume you made it home with no problems last night."

"Of course."

I'm pretty sure she just rolled her eyes, even though I can't see her.

"That's not why I called." Olivia pauses, and I know she's about to say something I'm not going to like. "Let me prove my theory to you. Introduce me to your grandfather."

I'm right. I hate it. I'm also not stupid enough to flat-out refuse her because if I do, I know she'll do something I'll like even less. "Why?"

"Take me to his home, point me in the right direction, and I will get you the proof."

"By stealing it?"

"By borrowing it. I'll hand it over to you as soon as I

find it and you can do with it what you want. But you have to promise to call off Vincenzo."

"And if the information doesn't prove your father's innocence?"

"It will. But if it doesn't, you can turn him over to the police."

"Just like that?"

"Yes."

Her confidence in her father is admirable, and I consider her offer in silence for several long seconds. I don't do it to keep her in suspense. I'm genuinely trying to decide the best course of action.

If I confront my grandfather, I don't believe he'll tell me the truth. He'll give me whatever I want to hear or whatever will best serve his purpose. I know because I'm just like him.

"Aiden? Are you still there?"

"So you'll be my own personal cat burglar?"

I hear something that sounds like a laugh filter though the phone.

"If it's in the house, I'll find it."

I have no doubt about her skill. I just don't want her anywhere near my grandfather. I don't want him to know what she looks like, I don't want her to talk to him. I don't want her in the same room with him. I also know if I don't take her, she'll go herself. And if she gets caught, my grandfather won't hesitate to have her arrested. Or worse.

"I'll arrange it for tomorrow night."

"What time?"

"Be at my home around seven."

"Okay."

She's gone before I can say anything else. I set the phone back on the desk and stare at it for a good minute. I'm still staring when my office door opens.

"Plotting more ways to make my life miserable?"

My father watches me with a look I've come to recognize. He wants something and today I'm in no mood to give him anything. I'm also in no mood to play nice.

"What do you want?"

Mark's eyebrows rise, as if he's hurt by my question. "Someone take away your favorite toy?" Sitting in the chair on the opposite side of the desk, he looks at me as if he's learned something new and interesting. Or he's found a chink in my armor. "Or did you finally fuck something up that you can't fix?"

The verbal sparring is nothing new. I usually get a perverted sense of enjoyment from it. Today, he's the perfect target to work out my frustration.

"Are you here for another handout? Do you need me to bail you out of another failed investment? What is it this time? The Russian hotel deal fall through? Or the film production company in L.A.? I forgot, those were last week. What is it this week?"

I expect him to huff and storm out. I'm kind of hoping he does. I'm already sick of dealing with him. Instead, he laughs and begins to clap. It's so unlike my father, I stare at him like I've never seen him before.

"Bravo, son. You finally found your claws."

Since this is probably the strangest conversation I've

had with my father in all the years I've known him, I stare at him as he smiles at me.

"What's your grandfather done to put that look on your face?"

"I don't know what you're talking about."

Mark's expression is smug. "Sure you do. Want to know how I know? Because I used to have that same expression after he'd cut me off at the knees. I knew you'd eventually be in the same position. I'm actually surprised it took this long."

Mark Battle has never truly acted like my father. He makes an effort with Giselle, mainly because she's a woman, and Mark sees her as weaker. He's completely wrong but Giselle no longer cares enough about him to let it get to her.

"Do you have a purpose for being here? No, wait. Even if you do, I don't really give a shit." I turn to my computer and dismiss him. "You know where the door is."

Out of the corner of my eye, I see him settle more deeply into the chair. I swallow a frustrated sigh but I'm pretty sure he knows exactly what he's doing.

"You know," Mark continues, "I once thought I wanted the seat you sit in. I thought if I worked hard enough and kissed his ass enough, my father would love me. I know how pathetic that sounds now. I also know that there are some things that just aren't worth the hassle. Are you finally learning that being his lackey is one of them?"

If I ignore him, eventually he'll get bored and go away. I try to concentrate on the rows of numbers on the computer screen but, as hard as I try, I can't get them to come into focus.

"So I'm curious."

Mark settles one ankle on a knee, his suit perfectly pressed, pant leg pulling up to show a sock that perfectly matches his suit. Today, that annoys the hell out of me. I've learned to dress and act like all of this matters, but I'm beginning to realize it doesn't, not at all.

"Did he finally ask you to do something that goes against your morals? Or has he shown you where all the bodies are buried?"

My head rears back as I glare at him and realize immediately I've made a tactical error. The conversation with Olivia left me unsettled, and Mark sees an opening to attack.

"I knew it had to be something like that. Want to talk about it?"

"Why the hell would I want to talk to you about anything?"

His smile takes me off guard. "Because we're a lot alike."

I open my mouth to tell him to fuck off but he continues on before I can.

"I was just like you at your age. Thought I knew everything. Thought I could handle anything he threw at me. And then he got my mother killed."

The shock I can't hide makes Mark's mouth curve with bitterness. "That man has no soul, Aiden. You have to have figured that out by now. You're a smart man. I also know how loyal you are to him. And that's my fault. When your mother dumped you on me, I had no desire to be a father."

I shake my head. "Are you dying? Are you trying to atone for being a shitty parent?"

Mark laughs and shakes his head. "No, though I can see why you might think that." Then he stands, and I stare at him like he's an alien and I've entered some strange alternate universe. "I have been a shitty parent. But you are still my son, Aiden. We will never see eye to eye, but here's a little fatherly advice you probably won't take. Get out now, while you still can. You're smart enough to do whatever the hell you want in life. Get out from under his thumb and get the fuck away from here. And never look back."

Then he walks out like he entered, in no hurry and as if he owns the place.

Leaving me to stare after him with questions I never expected to have.

TWENTY-FOUR

Olivia

I ARRIVE at Aiden's dressed in black but not my normal work clothes. Black slacks and a mostly black top with metallic threads running through it, cut low enough to reveal the tiny bit of cleavage I have.

Show a little tit and most men immediately lower your threat level. Yes, many men are that stupid. Especially men who think they're smarter than everyone else.

Aiden opens the door to my knock, sweeps his gaze down my body then back up to my face.

Aiden is not most men. He's smart but he's not easily distracted. And he knows what I'm capable of. Still, his gaze lingers a second longer on the bare skin of my chest than anywhere else before he meets my eyes again.

"I'm still not convinced this is the right course of action. Are you sure you want to do this?"

I hear what he's saying but I'm distracted because... Holy shit, Aiden in a suit is stunning.

He's wearing black, as well, with a white dress shirt but no tie. As if he came home from the office and I caught him in the act of undressing. Since I've seen him naked, I don't know why I find this sight almost as breathtaking.

It's like getting an illicit peek at a stranger.

And with his hair pulled back, I see what he'd look like if he would decide to take this whole businessman look seriously. And he's still seriously hot.

"Olivia?"

My gaze shoots back to his, and I nod. "Absolutely. Are you ready to leave?"

He doesn't move. "You look beautiful."

My eyes widen at his bald statement and my lips part but I'm not sure what to say.

"Thank you" is what finally emerges but now I'm flustered. That's not something I normally hear from men, at least not ones who aren't trying to pick me up in a bar. And then those are usually drunk and trying to get in my pants.

He nods and waves me into the house.

"I've called my grandfather to let him know I'm coming." We walk through the house to the kitchen, where he opens the door to the garage and waves me through. "I told him I needed to speak to him about something urgent and that I'd have a date with me."

Opening the passenger door to a big-ass Buick SUV, he helps me in, though I don't really need it. I take his hand because I'm an idiot, and I have a thing for his hands. They do wonderful things to my body.

When he climbs into the driver's seat and shuts the door, I get a whiff of aftershave and my mouth starts to water. Jesus, this has got to stop.

We're on the road seconds later and I realize I've been staring at him the entire time. Shaking my head, I tear my gaze away from him and stare out the front window.

"So you're going to keep him busy while I do my thing?"

His short laugh sounds a little sarcastic. "Exactly." He shakes his head, his mouth a straight line. "My grandfather is old school, wants everything on paper. He keeps everything related to business in his office at the back of the house. He has a computer but I've never seen him use it, and the only other person who has access to it is his personal assistant. Se's only allowed access when my grandfather's in the room with her. He trusts no one."

"I thought he trusts you."

"He does."

But Aiden no longer sounds as sure as he had before.

"I'm sorry."

He spares me a glance, his eyes narrowed. "What for?"

"That you no longer trust him. I know how that feels."

When he glances at me again, he's frowning. "What do you mean?"

"When Dad told me that he wasn't my biological father, I was devastated. He'd been lying to me my entire life, and I had a hard time with that. I hated him and my brothers. I even hated Maylyn because she actually is his biological daughter. It took me a while to realize that sometimes you hurt the people you love by keeping things from them that will hurt them."

"And you think that's what my grandfather does? That he hides things from me so I don't get hurt?" His laughter is definitely sarcastic now. "I gave up the idea that my grandfather has actual feelings years ago. When my mother dropped me on my father, he passed me off to my grandparents. I knew the only reason they kept me was because of my grandmother. She had a heart. The old bastard doesn't. But I'm grateful he didn't send me to foster care. He gave me everything I needed. Sent me to school, gave me a job. Hell, he gave me an empire. And when he's gone, it'll be mine. So he wasn't warm and fuzzy. I'm okay with that."

"And if it turns out to be true? That he's the reason your grandmother died?"

Aiden pauses, and I'm not sure he's going to answer. Finally, after at least a full minute of silence, he glances my way again.

"Then I'll put him in a dark hole and take his company. And I'll make sure he suffers every fucking day for the rest of his life."

I'm not shocked by the vehemence in Aiden's voice. I know how much his grandmother meant to him, even if he's never said the words. I can hear it in his voice every time he talks about her, in the look in his eyes.

He may come off as a stone-cold bastard but he does have feelings. And I'm probably a huge fool for thinking he has feelings for me other than lust. Blinking, I tear my gaze away from him and stare out the front window.

"Have I frightened you?"

His question isn't exactly a surprise, but I don't know how to answer. "No, I'm not frightened of you."

At least not in the way he thinks. I'm frightened that my growing feelings for him are going to make me even more stupid than I already feel.

"Then why do you look scared?"

I roll my eyes and hope that moves him away from that line of questioning. "I'm not scared. I'm thinking about what I need to do. Tell me more about the layout of the house."

As we drive, Aiden gives me the rundown on the layout, and I force myself to focus. By the time we pull up to the ostentatious mansion only a few miles from Aiden's home, I feel like I've got a pretty good idea of what I need to do.

But when I actually see the house, I'm a little awed.

"Damn, did he really build this to look like a castle?"

"He always told people he built it for my grandmother. But I'm pretty sure he built it for his ego."

I've pulled high-profile jobs before, broken into a few Society Hill homes that made my apartment look like a homeless person's makeshift tent. This place is on a totally different level.

"How the hell much money is he worth?"

"More than any person needs. But when you come from nothing, you get greedy. And you start to think you're owed it. So you push and you push and you never stop. You never get to the point where you think you have enough. You always want more."

"That's...sad. And a little sick."

Aiden's eyebrows rise and I realize he's talking about himself, as well as his grandfather. Then he shrugs.

"You're not wrong. It is a kind of sickness. Remember what I told you about the security system. The office has its own. You're going to have to disarm it before you can get in. Once you're in, the safe is in the floor in front of the desk. Unless he's had it replaced in the past year, it's an old-fashioned dial."

While they're not the easiest to crack without any of my usual equipment, they're not the hardest, either.

"I'm ready."

Aiden nods but doesn't get out of the car. "Don't get caught, Olivia."

"That's the plan."

"I'm not finished with you yet."

I'm not exactly sure if I should be flattered or pissed. I settle for confused and silent. In the next second, he turns and gets out of the car, leaving me blinking and shaking my head. By the time he opens the door to help me out, I manage to transform my expression into what I call bored socialite. I've never been one but I've seen enough of them to fake it. Just act like you don't give a shit about anyone or anything but yourself and are bored with everything around you. It's a good trick. People automatically dismiss you. Especially rich men.

"Don't stare." Aiden wraps his hand around my arm as we walk toward the front door.

"I'm not."

What I am doing is checking out the security setup.

Cameras covering all angles, windows wired. And if I'm not mistaken, bulletproof glass in the windows.

Overkill much? Jesus, this guy must think he's a king.

By the time Aiden rings the bell, I'm convinced I'm about to come face-to-face with royalty.

The arched wood door opens without a sound and a woman in a pressed black dress with white trim, looking straight out of a movie about England in the '50s, curves her lips just enough to suggest a smile.

"Mr. Knight. Mr. Battle is waiting in the white sitting room."

Oh hell, she even has a British accent. I find it hard not to laugh or shake my head. It's all so ludicrous. And Aiden grew up here? No wonder he's screwed up.

Why do you even care?

Trying to keep in character is going to require all of my attention so I force thoughts of Aiden out of my head and pretend to glance around the room. What I'm really doing is watching to see where the housekeeper goes.

According to what Aiden told me in the car, the house-keeper has her own rooms behind the kitchen, on the other side of the house from the office, which is where we seem to be heading.

I glance at Aiden, but he's staring straight ahead. His pace never falters, and he makes no concession for my shorter legs or the heels I rarely wear. I don't say anything, just let him pull me along.

When we reach our destination, I want to roll my eyes because, holy shit, she wasn't kidding. The room is almost completely white. It's like an anal retentive's wet dream. The white furniture sits directly in the center of the room. The white walls are a shade darker than the furniture. The glass side tables are perfect squares.

The place gives me the serious creeps.

And the man sitting on the black leather wing chair staring at the television on the far wall is so not what I expected.

I honestly didn't know what to expect but it's not a thin old man who looks too frail to walk. He doesn't immediately drag his gaze away from the television where he's watching what looks like a business news channel. I can't tell if he's watching the stocks scroll across the bottom or if he's listening to the talking head, who I'm pretty sure is speaking Japanese.

"Aiden. It's late. What do you want?"

No warmth in the man's voice at all. Nothing to indicate that Aiden is his grandson. Aiden doesn't seem put off at all. I'm cringing.

"We need to talk about the Saudi deal."

His grandfather's gaze barely glances over me before he says, "Send her out."

Aiden releases my arm but doesn't look at me. "Wait outside the door. I'll be out in a few minutes."

I blink, caught off guard by the coldness of his voice, but quickly fall back into character. With a shrug, I teeter back through the door, barely wincing when the door closes loudly behind me.

In the next second, I make a beeline for the closed door

across the hall. To the office. Exactly where Aiden said it would be. If someone's watching, it's game over anyway, so I don't even attempt to hide.

I head straight for the office.

TWENTY-FIVE

Aiden

"ARE you here to complain about Mark again, Aiden? I told you, you need to handle him. I'm not interested in your petty disputes with my son."

It was the perfect opening and the perfect distraction. And standing here staring at the man who'd raised me in his shadow, I knew what Olivia was going to find in that safe.

Nothing.

Because this old bastard was too smart to leave something so incriminating where I might be able to find it. I haven't been blind to the fact that he's a heartless bastard. I realized somewhere in my teens that he had very little capacity for emotion of any kind. The only things he loves are power and money. Things. Not people.

"Aiden." His voice snaps but he's lost the strength that

had kept me in line as a child and that made me think I wanted to be like him when I was a teenager. "What the hell's wrong with you? Why the hell are you wasting my time staring at me?"

Jesus, when did he get so old?

"No, it's not about Mark." I realize exactly what I need to say at this moment, what I should have said years ago. "It's time for you to step down."

His expression freezes, as if his brain is taking a second too long to process my statement. Then he begins to laugh, and I'm struck by the weakness in his voice. And by the hacking cough he develops that forces him to stop laughing and reach for the glass of water on the table beside him.

When he finally turns to glare at me, he looks even more pale than he did seconds ago.

"You forget your place. This isn't your company. It's mine. You're too damn cocky for your own good. I gave you too much responsibility. Now you think you can just force me to the side."

Sitting on the couch across from him, I stare at my grandfather and let myself really look. He's close to ninety years old although, until a couple of years ago, you would've thought he was closer to seventy. Tonight, he looks his age.

Why the hell have I allowed him so much control over my life? My only excuse is that, for so long, he's all I've had, the only remaining tie to my grandmother. And because I just didn't care about anything.

"It really was your fault, wasn't it? You're responsible

for her death. What did you do that got my grandmother killed?"

His face goes slack for several seconds before his eyes widen in shock. In the next second, he's sneering.

"Who the hell do you think you are? You don't get to question me. You don't have the right! You're nothing. The bastard son of a drug addict and a stupid rich boy. Anything you have I gave to you. I *made* you, Aiden."

I shake my head, forcing back my rising anger as much as I can. "You didn't make me, old man. I took every scrap of shit you gave me, and I turned it into gold. You haven't made one decision in the past five years that I haven't handfed you. You would've lost this company twenty times if I hadn't been here to stop you from making one awful deal after another."

"You don't know what you're talking about." His voice has been reduced to a hissing rasp that reveals a deep-seated hatred. "You're a gutter rat. Everyone knows that. You can put on a suit and a tie but you're still trash."

His words don't cut like they would have even six months ago. Instead, they only reinforce Olivia's assertion that he's responsible for my grandmother's death.

"I don't know why I've never seen it. Or maybe I have, and I made excuses for you."

"And maybe you're just like me, Aiden." Red mottles his cheeks and his eyes blaze with hatred. "Have you considered that?"

I have to give it to the bastard. His brain's still sharp after all these years. He knows exactly how to go for an opponent's jugular.

"Maybe I am. But then you should be worried. Because I know how you think. I know every move you can make. And I know how to take you down."

"One phone call." He's going hoarse, his voice raspy and thin. "That's all it'll take to have you thrown out on your ass."

"Are you so sure about that? Are you willing to bet your company on it? Because you haven't been into the office for...what? Six months? A year? The board deals with me on a daily basis. Every manager knows me by name. When was the last time you talked to any of them?"

I pause to let that sink in for several seconds, see the contemplation in his eyes. The realization that I'm right. Finally, I see a hint of fear in his eyes. I've got to hand it to the old bastard though. He covers it well as he leans back in his chair.

His expression clears, as if he doesn't have a care in the world. If I didn't know him better, I'd think he might have something on me, something he could use against me. But I've watched him work for years, studied his tactics, and learned how he operates. This is the part where he breaks people. People who don't know him, people who have secrets, they begin to sweat at this point.

Because if you have something to hide, you live in fear of someone finding out your secret. You have to be really good at deception to cover. And my grandfather is good. He's just not as good as he used to be.

"I'm in no danger of losing my company, Aiden, no matter what you might think. But you need to tread carefully here. I'm willing to forgive you for thinking you could manipulate me in some way. I guess I should be proud of you. I've taught you well."

"You taught me how to be ruthless, yes. You just never expected me to use it on you, did you?"

"You've got a long way to go before you can intimidate me, boy."

"I'm no longer a boy. I haven't been for many years. And that will be your downfall. You thought you could keep me contained, didn't you? Thought I'd always be under your thumb. And all this time, I never realized I was setting the groundwork for this, the night I'd tell you you're done."

His sneer returns but it doesn't hold the same power it has in the past. It makes me shake my head and wonder why I've let this go on for so long.

"You used her death to control me, used my grief to keep me in line. And I let you. No more."

"You don't have any idea what you're talking about. And you need to shut your mouth before you say another word about my wife."

"Is it because you got her killed that you don't like to talk about her, or did you really just not care about her? Was she just someone you slept with—"

"Shut your mouth!"

I do, but only because I realize I've won this round. And tomorrow, when I go to the office, I'll win the war.

Time to go.

I stand, already planning my strategy for tomorrow. For the past few minutes, I've forgotten that Olivia is doing my dirty work. Now, we need to leave but I don't know if

I've given her enough time to get back to where she's supposed to be waiting. And at this point, I don't care.

I take out my phone and text her, telling her to get out of there now. Behind me, I hear my grandfather rising from his chair.

"You don't want to cross me, Aiden. I still hold the power."

I spare him a glance over my shoulder. "Don't bother to show me out. I know where the door is."

"You're going to regret this, you ungrateful bastard. I will bury you."

"No, you won't. You can't. You set me up perfectly for this, and now I'm going to make you pay."

I head for the door while he struggles to keep up with me. He can't. He's old and weak and I'm more than able to outpace him. He's still calling my name as I head for the front door. I'm stone-cold rational, thinking more clearly than I have in years.

I see Olivia standing in the foyer. I can tell by the look on her face that she's confused and the slight shake of her head tells me she's found nothing.

Doesn't matter. I know all I need to.

I don't need her anymore. Our arrangement is over.

TWENTY-SIX

Olivia

I CAN SEE by the look on Aiden's face that something's happened.

Something that's changed the game.

He looks straight at me but I can tell he doesn't see me. I keep my mouth shut as he takes my arm and points me toward the front door. His text telling me to meet him now had surprised me. I'd been working on the safe and had two numbers cracked. The third had eluded me. I was starting to worry I wouldn't get it.

Then my phone vibrated, and I hustled out of the office to meet him in the hall. I can't completely control the shock on my face because Aiden's expression is furious. I've never seen him look as angry as he does now.

His hand tightens around my arm. I feel the restraint he's exercising. He doesn't want to hurt me, but he's fighting against the fury I see on his face. If I were on the receiving end of that look, I'd be terrified. I keep my mouth shut as we hustle toward the door. Aiden has his hand on the knob when I hear his grandfather call out.

"Aiden! Stop right there."

I glance over my shoulder and see Aiden's grandfather stalking up the hallway behind him.

Aiden ignores him, pulling open the door and urging me through it in front of him.

"Don't walk away from me. I will destroy you. You'll be out on your ass tomorrow morning. You'll have nothing."

Aiden turns on his heel so fast, I gasp, my eyes widening as he takes two steps forward. Then he stops, and his entire body stills. When he speaks, his voice holds a deadly serious tone that makes my stomach clench.

"No, you won't. Because I'll have everything you own." His voice barely rises above a whisper, but I can hear him perfectly. "I'll take it all because I'm the one in charge. I have been for years. You were too stupid to realize what I was doing. You're weak, old man. You're the only one who doesn't know it. No one will blink an eye when I tell them you've become too senile to be involved in running an empire. And if you try to cross me, I will tell everyone how you were the reason your wife was killed."

"You have no idea what you're talking about." Aiden's grandfather's voice cracks. Aiden's hit a vulnerable spot.

"Would you like to bet the rest of your life on that? Maybe a judge would go easy on you because of your age. Or maybe, when I present that second set of books you tried to cover up, he'll just lock you up and throw away the key. You won't be able to buy your way out of that. I'll make sure of it. And if you don't go to jail, I'll make damn sure you suffer every day for the rest of your life, knowing I've taken everything you've built."

When Aiden finally goes silent, all I can hear is his grandfather's raspy breath and the pounding of my heart.

I've been fooling myself these past few days. Foolish to think I could handle Aiden. That I was, in any way, an equal in ruthlessness or cunning. I have no idea what happened while I was trying to crack the safe but obviously something had. Something that made Aiden realize he has the upper hand on his grandfather and that he doesn't need my help to crush the old man.

He's perfectly capable of doing that all by himself.

When Aiden turns and begins to walk again, I go with him without complaint. I want out of here and I want out now. He doesn't say a word as he helps me into the car. I'm too lost in thought to care. As far as I know, he doesn't have the second set of books. But I'm not sure of anything anymore.

He doesn't speak until we're well under way.

"Did you find anything?"

His question comes out of the blue. I blink out of the fugue I've been in.

"What?"

"Did you find anything in his office?"

I swallow hard because I have no idea how he's going to react. I'm not frightened of him. I guess I should be. I really know nothing about him. And everything I thought I knew has been blown away in the space of five minutes.

"I didn't have time to look."

He nods, as if that's exactly what he expected to hear.

And I take a deep breath. "I don't think I'm up for a night out. I...want to go home."

His jaw clenches, and I expect him to tell me no.

Instead, he nods. "Probably for the best. I have work to do tonight."

I consider my next question carefully but I have to ask.

"Are you going to call off Vincenzo?"

He slides me a glance. "I already have."

Oh.

"Did you think I wouldn't keep my word?"

His softly voiced question makes me think. Had I doubted him?

No, I hadn't. Until I heard him tell his grandfather he was going to crush him. Then, I saw a man I hadn't seen before. A man completely capable of being ruthless.

"No, I didn't doubt you."

"But now you do. Are you frightened of me now, Olivia? Do you finally see the man I really am?"

Confusion makes me shake my head but not in answer to his questions. I shouldn't be having such a hard time reconciling this man with the man I've let fuck me over the past several days. Maybe I saw something in his personality that just isn't there. Maybe I led myself to believe he was a different person so I could justify the sex. The sex I enjoyed.

Maybe—

No. No more maybes.

I keep my mouth shut for the rest of the drive home. Thankfully it's not far because I feel like my head's about to explode. My temples throb and my lungs hurt as Aiden pulls up beside my car.

There's a pit in the bottom of my stomach that's making it hard for me to breathe. I find myself staring at his profile, his jaw clenched tight. I want to run my fingers along that firm line, feel the scruff against my fingers.

I sense his seething frustration and anger and want to ease it. Even though I know I can't. That he probably doesn't want me to. He's done with me. When he turns to me, I quickly look away and reach for the door handle.

His hand on my arm keeps me glued to my seat.

"Nothing you heard tonight should be repeated."

I know he has to say it, but it still puts me on edge.

"I'm not stupid."

"No, you're not. You're also a thief and if the information is worth enough money, you may be tempted to sell it."

The urge to say something equally as hurtful makes my jaw ache. I bite my tongue because I know anything I say right now will be wrong. It'll betray the hurt that's tying my stomach in knots.

God, I'm so stupid. He's not allowed to hurt me. Not like this. How could I allow this to happen?

I wait for him to say something else, though I have no idea what that would be. Is this it? Do I get out of the car and walk away and forget any of this ever happened? Can I forget? I don't have a clue. When he stays silent, I turn and grab the door handle and slide out of the car.

"Olivia."

With my feet on the ground, I feel a little more stable. But the minute my gaze meets his, I know I'm going to hate the next words out of his mouth.

"Consider our arrangement fulfilled."

I bite back the harsh words on the tip of my tongue, the ones that would reveal much more about my feelings right now than I want him to know. Instead, I take a step away from the truck and shut the door. I expect him to pull away, but the SUV doesn't move. Turning, I head for my car. It takes me two tries to get the key in the ignition. When I finally do, I rev the engine and peel out of the driveway and I never look back.

By the time I get to my building, I'm pissed off. Utterly and completely furious. And sick to my stomach. I take a few deep breaths, trying to calm myself. I don't want to be alone. Turning from my door, I walk back down a flight of stairs to Bryant's apartment.

He answers my knock with raised eyebrows, which immediately slam down when he sees my face.

"What the hell happened and who do I need to beat?"

I can't even conjure a smile. I just shake my head and walk by him when he steps aside. Heading straight for his fridge, I pull out two beers and hold one over my shoulder for him as he comes up behind me.

"Liv."

The tone of his voice makes tears sting the corners of my eyes. I twist the cap off the beer before I turn and take a swig. Bryant watches me like a hawk.

"What's wrong, little sister?"

He says the one thing he knows will break through my silence. Reese and I may be closer, but Bryant takes his position as oldest as seriously as a heart attack.

"We need to check with Vincenzo, but I'm pretty sure Dad's safe now."

Bryant doesn't respond right away. He takes a long pull on his beer before he sets the bottle on the counter.

"What'd you have to do to make that happen?"

"Nothing I didn't want to do."

"That doesn't make me feel better." His voice has dropped into growl territory. "Talk to me, Liv."

"The guy I told you about, the one I was supposed to steal the file from, he's the one behind everything. He set it all up. He blamed Dad for his grandmother's death, but he realized it wasn't Dad's fault."

Bryant takes another swallow of beer, and I know he's thinking this through. "So now he's over it all? Just like that?"

"He told me Dad doesn't have anything more to worry about."

"But you're not sure this guy will keep his word?"

"No...I mean, yes, I think he'll keep his word. I just..."

I sigh and try to find the words I need, but they elude me. I don't want to reveal too much but I need Bryant to understand. And to not ask too many questions because I really am afraid he'll go after Aiden with a baseball bat. And if anyone's going to smack Aiden, I want it to be me.

"Just what? Come on, Liv, spit it out."

"I think...I fell for the mark."

I'm pretty sure I've stunned Bryant into silence. His

lips part but he doesn't say anything and he stares at me with his eyes wide. After a few seconds, his eyebrows lower and his mouth becomes a tight, straight line.

"If he touched you—"

"It's not like that." I hurry to cut him off. I don't want him to think too hard about anything else. "This is a stupid girl thing, and I needed someone to know. Reese would fly off the handle and Maylyn would tell me to pursue it and—"

"And you know I'm going to tell you what you need to hear." Bryant shakes his head. "You need to forget this guy and stay as far away from this as possible from here on out. If Dad's clear, you don't need to be involved anymore. I didn't want you involved in this in the first place. Now that it's over, you need to get out. Do you think this guy will come after you?"

I shake my head. "I don't think he wants anything to do with me."

"Then that's a good thing."

I should agree. I don't want Bryant to freak out. But I don't want to lie. I want to cry on my brother's shoulder. And I know I can't. So I nod and stare down at my beer, trying not to let the tears gathering at the corners of my eyes fall.

We stand in silence for several long seconds. I can practically feel the restraint Bryant is using to keep from speaking. Finally, he sighs. I tense, expecting him to ask more questions.

Instead, he puts his hand on my shoulder and squeezes. "Since you're here, you wanna watch that show you keep telling me about? That one with all that freaky shit and all those characters who share a brain?"

A laugh catches me off guard and I look up at my bad-ass brother, who's just asked if I want to watch *Sense8*. My brother, who normally wouldn't be caught dead watching any show that didn't have bikers, gangsters, and at least two bloody killings per show.

I nod and smile and take his hand when he reaches for mine and drags me toward his couch.

And for the next four hours, we drink beer and watch TV as he sacrifices his bed, and I fall asleep with my head on his thigh because I don't want to go home.

TWENTY-SEVEN

Aiden

"THIS HAS to get to the board members this morning. I need you to make sure it gets into their hands personally."

Lifting her gaze from the computer screen to meet mine, Jeannie swallows hard, her eyes wide. But she's pure professionalism when she nods.

"Of course. I'll make sure they go to personal emails and immediately do a follow-up call."

"I'm sure there're going to be questions so prioritize my morning schedule. Those calls are top of the list. I expect there'll be a lot. Start funneling them through as soon as you get them. I want this handled as quickly as possible."

"Yes, sir. Of course."

She pauses, her expression a study in indecision. She wants to say something but she's not sure she should.

"Jeannie, whatever you want to say, just say it. I trust you. I hope you trust me."

Her eyes widen even more. "Oh, I do. It's just... I don't know whether to say congratulations or condolences. I know you and your grandfather are close, and I don't know if this means he has health issues or if he's died or if he just decided to step back and let you take the reins."

Shit. How the hell did I not realize the board would need a solid reason to replace my grandfather? This is the one reason they will all agree on. "And this is why you're about to get a raise. He's still breathing, but he's no longer mentally competent."

After a quick modification, which makes her give me a sad little smile, I watch her send out each of the six letters individually. Then I retreat to my office and wait for the calls to pour in. I'm sure they will. I'm also fairly certain my grandfather has already been on the phone with most of the board members this morning so I'm expecting to get pushback. A lot of pushback.

The board members mainly know me as the bastard interloper, the man who pushed out his own father to get control of the company. I'm hoping that, even if they don't like me, they realize how much I've done to move this company forward. How much shit I've shoveled, how many sacrifices I've made, how many lines I've crossed.

And the one thing they don't know that's been the worst.

Forcing Olivia into a relationship then being forced to give her up.

I know she thought I was angry with her last night. I

wasn't. Not with her. I was furious at myself for falling for my grandfather's bullshit. For his involvement in my grandmother's death. And for the fact that, if I want to take this company away from my grandfather, I need laser focus. She's a distraction I can't afford.

Not to mention the fact that, if the board finds out I'm dating a thief, I'll be out on my ass.

And would that be a bad thing?

The subversive voice in my head makes me grit my teeth in anger but I stomp it down. I can't deal with it today. I have too much else on my plate.

No, I did the right thing last night. I can't have my attention split right now, and Olivia is the biggest distraction I've ever met. She's a thief, and I'm staging a hostile coup of a multinational, multibillion-dollar organization... whose former CEO could decide to air our dirty laundry in the press and bring the whole damn company down.

I wouldn't put it past him. I'm banking on the fact that the board won't let it happen, won't let him ruin their profit margin. I'll do everything I can to head it off, but it's not going to be pretty, and it's not going to be easy. I don't have the possibility of seeing Olivia at the end of the day as incentive to get through.

She probably hates me, would probably like to take her little pocketknife to my throat and tell me to go fuck myself. Damn it. Why the fuck does that make me horny?

Because you wanted more than a quick fuck.

No, I didn't. At least it didn't start out that way. And it's probably better if she stays away from me. Better for both of us.

Which just makes me even more pissed off than I already am.

Is she happy to be rid of me?

Christ. What the fuck is wrong with me? I need to stop thinking with the little head in my goddamn pants and use my brain to hold on to what I'm trying to take.

And will it be worth it?

It has to be because it's all I've got.

When the first call comes through, I'm ready for a fight.

THE KNOCK on the door doesn't sound like Jeannie's but I say, "Come in," before I think about it.

"What's up, Jeannie?" I glance up, and my eyes widen with shock. "What the hell do you want?"

My father strolls through the door, smile on his face, as if he holds the secrets to the universe.

"I understand congratulations are in order. I came to offer mine."

I have never trusted my father, and now doesn't seem like the time to start.

"You didn't answer my question. What do you want?"

He holds up his hands, as if to show me he has nothing to hide. I don't expect him to be holding a dagger, but I do expect he has a figurative one somewhere in hiding.

"That's actually the only reason I'm here, though I know you won't believe me. Your coup was bloodless and completely unexpected. I applaud you. I'm sure your grandfather is spitting bullets at the moment."

My jaw clenches against the urge to tell him to go to hell. I should ignore him. I've been on the phone for most of the morning, fielding questions and concerns from the board members.

I'd expected a lot more pushback and a lot more sniping and backstabbing. What I got was a lot of questions and unexpected support from almost everyone. The two holdouts want a face-to-face meeting tonight over dinner.

That's the kind of shit my father usually handles. And I have to give him credit. He handles it well. He's good at it. I could probably learn a thing or two from him. Which means I need him to do something for me.

"I'm meeting Gable and Carson tonight for dinner. I want you there."

The shock on Mark's face coaxes a quick smile out of me before I rein it in. He's not as fast but he does manage to school his expression into something resembling cool interest.

"I'm happy to help in any way you need. What time and where?"

My turn to be shocked. I expected him to give me a hassle or, at the very least, be a prick about it. So, of course, I figure he's playing an angle, which means I need to keep my guard up tonight.

After I give him the details, he nods. "I think you should invite Giselle as well. Having her there will be a show of strength. With the three of us, your grandfather can't claim we're not united, and Gable and Carson won't be as likely to think they can find a chink in the armor."

My shock continues to grow. So does my suspicion. My father does nothing out of the kindness of his heart. Obviously, he wants something. The idea of inviting Giselle is a good idea, which I plan to follow through on. Otherwise...

"What do you want in return?"

Mark's grin is a little rueful. "You'll never cut me any slack, will you?" He didn't give me a chance to answer. "Not that I expect it or deserve it. I wasn't there for you, not when you were born, not growing up. However, I should point out that if I hadn't dumped you on your grandfather, you wouldn't be in this position."

My eyebrows rise. "So I should thank you for being an absolute asshole?"

He shrugs. "Of course not. I just want you to know that you come by it honestly."

That dig hits too close to home and I clench my jaw against the urge to tell him to go to hell. And confirm his statement.

"So why should I trust you to help me tonight?"

I conveniently forget that he didn't offer to go with me tonight. I told him he was going.

"You're good at dealing with the business, Aiden, but you're not a people person. You don't do interpersonal well. The only person you get along with is your sister. You're a bulldozer and that's not what you need to handle this situation."

Because he's actually making sense, I don't interrupt.

"You need me to smooth the way. Gable and Carson

have been with your grandfather the longest. They still look at you and see an outsider. You need your sister to soften your edges. You make those bastards enough money that they can overlook the fact that you're not one of them. But don't make the mistake of thinking they'll ever accept you as an equal. To them, you're a necessary evil. Let me and your sister handle them. You just sit and glare at them. They'll fall into line."

He makes it sound like the easiest thing in the world. Just give him the power to represent me, and everything will be fine. We'll be one big happy family and every slight of the past will be forgiven.

Huge load of bullshit. But he does have a good point about the board members. With him to smooth the way, I'll have less resistance.

Or I could tell my father to fuck off and force the board members' hands at dinner. I'll lay out the new world order and tell them to get on board or get the hell out of my way because this transition is happening with or without them. And if they don't like it, well, tough shit.

"Why the hell should I believe a word that comes out of your mouth?"

He doesn't flinch or falter, just continues like he's had this speech prepared for days and not hours.

"Because I have absolutely nothing to gain." He shrugs, like it's no big deal. "My father handed you his company on a silver platter then gave you the ability to cut him off at the knees and shove him out the door. I have no doubt that you hold all the cards here. I'm simply willing to do what I can to make the transition easier because at the end of the day, what's good for the company is good for me."

There it was. His end game. Money. That's what it all boils down to with Mark. And I understand. Because that's all that matters, right? The bottom line. I still hesitate. Do I really hate Mark so much that I'm willing to put the future of the company on the line just to spite him?

And if I let him speak for me tonight, does that show weakness? Do I really need him and Giselle to smooth the way? I want to tell him to fuck off, to take his offer and shove it.

"Make the arrangements."

Mark can't hide his shock completely but he covers it quickly. Nodding, he rises from the chair and heads for the door.

"I'll get right on that. I'll tell Giselle to meet us at Haven at seven. I'll have Gable and Carson join us at eight."

He disappears through the door, my mind racing. Everything in my world has turned upside down and I'm no longer sure which way is up. My life has never been normal. And what the hell is normal, anyway?

Why can't I make my own normal?

Because you fucked up the one thing that might have been yours.

It wouldn't have worked anyway.

If I keep telling myself that, maybe I'll eventually believe it.

TWENTY-EIGHT

Olivia

"I HAVE a job I think you may want."

I'm sitting next to Maylyn on the couch in my dad's house, watching Buffy on well-worn DVDs. They'd been mine before I passed them on to my sister. I can recite most of seasons one and two. We're on season four, and I've been watching half-heartedly.

I've been in a funk for the past five days and I know my family's been worried. But I haven't been able to climb out of it. And I'm ignoring all the reasons why. When my phone rang, I'd grabbed it so Maylyn didn't try to take it and turn it off so it wouldn't interrupt the show.

Now, I frown because I hadn't been expecting to hear from the private detective who occasionally books my services for clients. He's based in Washington DC but has an office in Philly. My dad had hooked me up with Pete a few years ago, and I'd done several jobs for him. Very profitable jobs.

"Oh yeah? Why is that?"

Sliding off the couch, I motion to my sister, letting her know I'm going into the next room. She barely notices I'm going.

"Because it's in the city, and it's pretty straightforward. Office building, standard security, get the file, get out."

He's right. It's exactly the type of job I excel at. "When?"

"Well, that's the kicker. Client needs it to happen tomorrow night."

Of course.

Sighing, I shake my head, though I know he can't see me. I'm really not in the mood to pull another job but I also don't want to turn down work. You never know when the next one will come along.

"Okay, Pete. Send me the information."

"I knew I could count on you, kid. Sending the file now. Talk to you day after tomorrow to arrange pickup."

Hanging up to the chime of a new email, I pull up the file. I don't recognize the address, but I know it's downtown. He's also sent the security protocols and building specs. Everything I need to pull this on short notice.

"New job?"

I turn to find Maylyn leaning against the open doorway between the living room and the dining room where I'd retreated to talk to Pete.

Smiling, I nod and try to make it real. "Gotta pay the bills. Pete says it's an easy one."

"Are they ever easy?"

Her question is deadly serious and so is her expression and I realize I'm about to be cross-examined. Maylyn's been quiet all night. She must've been biding her time.

"Not really, no."

"Dad's not home. Are you going to tell me what happened? I'm worried about you, Liv. Something's going on with you."

"It's nothing—"

"Don't." She shakes her head. "Don't lie to me. If you don't want to talk, just tell me. But Liv... Are you okay?"

Maylyn's question isn't unexpected, but her tone is so worried, I feel tears well. And that sucks. I've been holding it together since the night Aiden showed his true colors. Mostly. I guess. Then again, maybe I haven't been hiding it enough.

"I'm fine." I hold up my hand when she opens her mouth to contradict me. "I am. I'm just...angry at myself. I made a tactical error. I trusted someone I shouldn't have. It happens. I'm moving on."

Maylyn's eyebrows rise. "Uh-huh. From this angle, it doesn't look like there's much moving on going on."

I have the almost uncontrollable urge to stick my tongue out at her. I rein it in and shrug instead. "I don't know what else to tell you."

"Why don't you start by telling me who the guy is?"

"No one you know."

"Which is curious because I don't remember you saying you had a date, like, in the last year."

"That's bullshit, by the way. I've been on dates in the past year."

"None that've led to a second date." Maylyn sighs. "What happened on this last job? That's what this is about, isn't it?"

Of course it is, and I know I shouldn't open my mouth. I don't want to burden my sister with this crap or tell her how much of an idiot I was. Especially since it's in the past now and I'm over it.

And that's such a load of crap. I'm not over it. I'm still so pissed off at Aiden, I can't even think about him without gritting my teeth. And getting teary-eyed. Which just makes me even more pissed off.

"Liv?"

I meet Maylyn's concerned gaze and force a smile. "I was so stupid."

"You're one of the smartest people I know. If this guy doesn't see that then he's an asshole and he's not worthy of you. I sincerely hope you told him to go fuck himself."

I start to laugh because it's all I can do. I'm tired of feeling weepy over Aiden. Tired of missing a man who dropped me without a second glance. The whole damn thing had been doomed from the start, like some Nicholas Sparks book where someone always dies.

"I wish I had."

Maylyn shrugs, her expression flippant but fierce. "Then you should. Just stand in front of him and tell him to take a flying leap. I'll even go with you."

"I think this is something I should do on my own. But I appreciate your moral support."

"Family first. Always."

The words are our dad's, but we all live by them. Those words bind us together.

"Always." I pause, looking for words that won't seem like I'm trying to excuse his behavior, even though Maylyn has no idea what Aiden and I had agreed to. "Aiden doesn't understand. He doesn't have a true family, not like ours. He doesn't have anyone to protect his back."

"Sounds like you're making excuses for him."

Grimacing, I shake my head. "No, I'm not. It's just... I don't know. I guess I thought maybe there was a connection there that wasn't."

"So if he called you tomorrow, you wouldn't give him the time of day?"

Would I?

My silence is all the answer my sister needs.

"Whoa. Okay, maybe you do need an intervention. Or a vacation. Very, very far away. Or you need to tell this dude he's an idiot and to get his head out of his ass."

"I love you, Lynnie, but you know what I do for a living. He runs a legitimate company. And I'm not all that legitimate."

She shrugged like it was no big deal. "No one's perfect."

The simplicity of her statement makes me shake my head again. "It's never that easy."

She rolls her eyes. "Well, duh. Nothing's ever easy. But

sometimes you just gotta say 'fuck it' and go after what you want."

"And if what you want doesn't want you back?"

Maylyn's lip curled into a sneer and the look on my baby sister's face could scare off a grown man. "Then he's a dick, and we'll send Bryant and Reese to kick his ass."

"Don't you think I can fight my own battles?"

"Of course you can. So why aren't you?"

THE NEXT NIGHT, I'm still considering Maylyn's last question as I approach the building for the job I took from Pete.

I waver back and forth between telling myself to move on and wondering what Aiden's doing then telling myself to move on again because I'm pretty sure he's not even thinking about me. I can only imagine what he did with the information he discovered about his grandfather's role in his grandmother's death. I doubt he'll ever go public with any of it, so I don't figure I'll ever really know.

But I was curious enough to check the business news networks the next day to see if any of them mentioned Aiden. Of course, none of them did. I know enough about Aiden to know he likes working behind the scenes.

Hoodie up as I stroll by the building I need to crack, I note the security guards exactly where they should be at this time of night. Watching the closed-circuit security feed at the desk in the lobby, which I can clearly see as I pass by.

The building is like all the others on the street. A high-rise with top-of-the-line security and two guards who're vigilant but a little too confident in their tech. Since I'm in the heart of downtown and it's after ten p.m. on a Tuesday night, there aren't a lot of people strolling by on the sidewalk. I stick out by virtue of being in the area at night when no one else is working. The fact that I look like a college student taking a shortcut home after night classes at Penn helps.

The tricky part is going to be getting into the building undetected. Pete's already given me the best access point. Back of the building, service entrance, only accessible if you have the code for the door and know the location of the access.

The cameras back here are motion-activated. At this time of night, if I maneuver correctly, I can get to the door without setting off the detectors. And if I'm faster still, I can get inside before anyone notices the door opening and closing.

Lot of luck involved but I'm good at my job. Just not good at anything else apparently.

Shaking off that thought, I make it through the door without setting off any alarms and head for the stairs. I have to get to the twentieth floor so I start the climb, head down. If the guards actually catch sight of me on the security feed, they won't see my face.

Not even winded by the time I get to the right floor, I'm in the zone now and happy to be there. I'd been a little worried all this shit with Aiden would screw with my ability to work. Nice to know it didn't.

I make it to my target in a matter of minutes. I stare at the door to the office, feeling confident that I can be in and out without being seen. But something about the name on the door catches my eye and makes me pause. Something about the way it looks. I'd researched the company, found nothing to make me suspicious of...what?

Do you really think he'll go out of his way to set up another meeting?

Do I want him to?

Shit. This is how you make mistakes and get your ass caught.

Pushing thoughts that don't belong there out of my head, I take one last look around, double-check the position of the cameras, and head for the door. Sliding into the office, I lean against the wall and just breathe for a few seconds. Even if security caught sight of me, it'll take them several minutes to get up the elevator. So I'd better get moving.

What I need is in the office in the back, so I head for the door at the far end of the room. As I get closer, the hair on the back of my neck lifts and goosebumps cover my arms.

Someone's in the office. Don't ask me how I know. I just do.

And I think I know who it is. If I'm wrong, I'll be arrested. If I'm right...

I should leave. Get out now.

Anger burns its way through my body, spreading out from my gut until I'm pretty sure steam curls from my ears. That damn logo on the door. I realize it looks familiar because it is. It resembles the Battle Holdings logo. Aiden's company.

Coincidence? No way in hell.

Forgoing stealth, I fling open the door and step into the dark office. Except it's not an office. There's no desk, just three couches in a U-shape and two chairs at the ends. If I could see more clearly, I'm pretty sure it'd look *Mad Men* chic. But my attention is fully focused on the dark figure sitting on the couch at the far end of the room.

And I stop because something's not right. No, that's not it. Something's different.

"Aiden?"

The man sitting in the dark doesn't answer right away and for a few seconds, I'm frozen. I was so certain he's here—

"Shut the door behind you, Olivia."

My breath releases in a rush. It is Aiden. There's no mistaking that voice. Or what it does to me, which makes the anger overtake the fear.

"Turn on a light first."

I hear him huff out a laugh then light flashes across the room, and when my eyes finally adjust, I see what I registered as different.

"You cut your hair."

His mouth twists into what you can almost call a grin. "Thanks to you, I now have control of one of the largest Fortune 500 companies in the world. I decided I should look the part."

He looks...amazing. Like he walked off a *GQ* photo shoot. His hair isn't short, but it doesn't reach his shoulders. I could still run my fingers through it and grab hold. My hands curl into fists so I can't reach for him.

"Congratulations. You look like a cutthroat tycoon. But you didn't need the haircut. You only had to make a demand and everyone in the room would know they had to jump to do your bidding."

"So you like it?"

My mouth drops open. "Are you seriously digging for a compliment from me?"

He shrugs one broad shoulder, but his gaze never leaves mine. "I figured we'd start with the easy stuff."

"Start what? And nothing has ever been easy between us."

His gaze darkens. "True."

"Then why am I here? You made it pretty clear we were finished. And I'm not stupid enough to make another deal with you. Once bitten, twice shy. You don't get a second bite."

"Not even out of your beautiful breasts?"

Heat blooms in my lower body, spreading outward and fueled by the blatant carnality of his statement and his expression. Damn him. But I wasn't kidding. I can't afford to let him get to me again. There's no future here. I don't trust him.

"What do you want?"

He pauses, and I hold my breath.

"Has your father had any more trouble with Vincenzo?"

The abrupt change in the direction of the conversation

makes me frown. "No. Why? Should we be worried that you didn't hold up your end of the bargain?"

"Not an ounce of give in you, is there?"

His expression is hard, but he sounds almost upset. My problem is I want to forgive him. I want to cover the space between us and sit on his lap and kiss him until my core aches then stick my hands down his pants and—

"I can't trust you."

His gaze remains steady on mine. "Did I break a promise to you, Olivia? Did I fail to uphold some part of our bargain?"

"The bargain was bullshit to begin with. You wanted to hurt my father by fucking me. But my dad wasn't the problem, was he? You're the one with the problem."

I expect him to get angry or to shut me down. Instead, he nods.

"You're right. So I'm here to offer you another bargain."

I shake my head. "No—"

"Come to dinner tomorrow night."

"Why would I do that?"

"Because you know you want to."

He's not wrong. And that's the best reason for staying away from him.

"And what do you want, Aiden? Just another fuck? I'm sure you can get that from anyone you meet. You don't need a woman to climb into your third-floor window. Or does that get you off?"

"You get me off."

God, the man's voice should be illegal. "So I'm just supposed to forget what you did?"

"No. But I'm hoping we can move on."

"Are you serious?"

"Yes."

"And if I say no?"

"You walk out the door."

"No strings?"

"No strings."

I turn and walk out the door.

TWENTY-NINE

Aiden

"ALL RIGHT, this moping has gone on long enough. You need to get your ass out of that house tonight and come with me." Giselle's voice rings through the phone, making me smile as it usually does. "I want you to meet me at Haven tonight. I want you to meet this—"

"No. Stop right there. I'm not meeting another one of your friends tonight. I agreed to meet your friend Wednesday night and that turned out to be a disaster."

A long-suffering sigh comes through. "You're totally right. That one's on me. I've apologized several times. I had no idea Vivian was such a flake. I mean the woman's a lawyer, for chrissake."

"She's also the most boring person I've ever met."

"I know. I'm sorry. But really Jenn's not at all—"

"No."

Another sigh. "So what are you going to do tonight besides watch the foreign markets and listen to horrible music?"

"Zeppelin is one of the best rock bands ever."

"Blah, blah, more boring stuff. And I notice you didn't say I was wrong about watching the foreign markets. Aiden, I'm worried. For the past two weeks, all you've done is work. You need to get a life, or you will turn into our grandfather, bitter and mean and a totally gross human being."

I'd told Giselle everything I'd learned about our grandfather in the two weeks since I'd taken the company. She hadn't been shocked. She'd been more shocked when I'd told her about Olivia. Hell, I'd shocked myself. And when I'd told Giselle the whole story, I thought she'd lump me in with our grandfather.

She hadn't. She'd told me I was an asshole and no wonder Olivia wouldn't see me again.

"Fine. Be all silent and broody. I knew you'd say no. Try not to spend all night working, Aiden." She pauses and I think she wants to say something else but all she says is, "Love you."

"Love you too. Be good tonight."

"No way in hell."

She hangs up, leaving me shaking my head.

And feeling guilty as my gaze turns to the television, where I have the BBC business news streaming. She's right. I need to get out. I can already feel the walls starting to close in around me, but there always seems to be something I need to handle personally. Maybe in a few years, it'll be different but now that I'm actually in charge, the weight on my shoulders seems a hell of a lot heavier.

And lonelier.

There's only one woman I have any desire for, and she turned and walked away from me a week ago and never looked back. I've had enough on my plate to keep me busy all week, and while business never really takes a break, this is Saturday night—

A noise from above catches my ear and my heart starts to pound out a harder beat. Which is ridiculous.

It can't be.

I gave her my word I wouldn't pursue her, that she could walk away, and I wouldn't follow. And when she left, not going after her was probably the hardest thing I've ever done. I'd been trained by my grandfather to take what I want and that you failed only because you didn't try hard enough so try again until you succeed.

So what the hell—

I hear distinct footsteps now and I head for the stairs to the second floor. The light shines at the end of the hall. I know I hadn't turned it on earlier.

Who the hell is in my bedroom?

Giselle was right about one thing. I've been miserable all week, and almost everyone who knows me has stayed far away if they didn't absolutely have to talk to me. Whoever has the absolute bad timing to break into my home tonight is about to find out just how bad my mood has been.

Stalking down the hall, I make no effort to hide my approach. I throw open the door, ready to expend some of this restless energy on the idiot in my bedroom, and stop in the doorway.

Olivia sits on the edge of the bed, legs dangling over the side, hands on her thighs, staring straight at me. She's wearing the same tight black leggings and skintight black shirt she wore the first night we'd met.

My breath catches in my throat. I'm struck momentarily dumb. For a man who needs to have the right words at all times, right now, they're eluding me.

I want to grab her and tie her to the bed so she can't get away but I know that's not going to get me what I want. Which is her.

So I plant my feet on the floor and cross my arms over my chest. And her lips curl in a way that makes my blood sizzle.

"What are you doing here?" My voice sounds tough. Hard. Exactly like it should.

"I've been told we need to talk."

What the hell? "Told by whom?"

"She told me she was your sister."

Giselle? "What did she want with you?"

On slim shoulder lifts then falls. "She said your grandfather wanted her to track me down. That he thought I might be useful as a weapon against you. I guess you do have an ally in your family. Giselle said she hoped I could talk some sense into you because you were...how did she say it?"

She taps a finger against her lips and my hands clench at my sides because I want to replace that finger with my mouth.

"Basically, she said you were a miserable ass and obviously pining over a woman. She hoped I was the right woman and that I'd pull you out of your funk."

"And what do you think?"

"I think she doesn't know what she's talking about."

"Then why are you here?"

"Call me curious."

"Just curious? Curious enough to break into my home. You know you could have come through the front door."

She shrugs and draws her legs up to cross them in front of her. "I like a challenge. You probably should lock that window."

"Maybe I left it open because I hoped someone would use it."

She doesn't respond right away, just sits there staring at me. I don't know what she's searching for, but I hope like hell she finds it.

"I may be willing to use the front door next time."

I force back a smile at the "next time" comment. "Do you want to suggest a mutually agreeable arrangement?"

Her lips twitch into a smile. "First, I want to know why you've been so miserable. You made the man responsible for your grandmother's death pay for his sins. You've taken his company, made yourself supreme leader of his universe."

My mouth twitches at her deliberate taunts. "I have. But I may have lost more than I gained. Unless you're here to tell me otherwise."

Another pause, then she crooks her finger at me. I don't hesitate. I cross the room and stand in front of her. Her lips are level with my chest, and if I rip my shirt over my head, she could use her mouth on my nipples. And if I push her back onto the bed, I could go to my knees, strip her naked and put my mouth on her sex and make her come around my tongue.

"I'm here to see if you're willing to make amends."

I'm on my knees in the next second, my hands around her waist, dragging those tight leggings off her body. Either she wasn't wearing underwear, or I took them along with the pants. Doesn't matter. They're gone, and she's bare from the waist down.

Holding her body by the hips, I look up into her eyes as she reaches for my head with one hand. I expect her to pull me in and I'm not against obeying that command. But she doesn't. She winds her fingers into my hair and her gaze follows her fingers.

"I do like it. You look...more civilized."

I give her the only answer I can. I show her just how uncivilized I still am. I draw my hands down to her thighs, spreading them farther. Then I lean forward and lick through her folds to her clit. Her thighs shake under my hands and her fingers tug at my hair. Hard. The sting feels so damn good.

"Aiden."

I fucking love hearing my name come out of her mouth in that breathy tone. It pushes me to go after her harder.

She tastes sweet and hot, and when she releases my hair and falls back onto the bed, her hips thrust forward, pressing her even closer to my face.

I sense her surrender and victory slams through me.

My cock, hard as granite, pushes against the zipper of my jeans.

"God, Aiden. Make me come."

That's exactly the plan and I use my tongue as my tool, lightly flicking her clit, teasing her unmercifully, before I stiffen it and lick inside her to fuck her with it. Squirming against me, she's heat and fire. I can barely hold her steady and I'm not sure I want to.

Her every move incites me. She's the piece of this puzzle that's been missing in the past week since I've taken over from my grandfather. Everything else is just business, but not Olivia. Not even when she broke into my house that first time. I need to make her scream my name. Need her to give herself over to me completely. To trust me.

Seconds later, she tenses, and I feel her quiver around my tongue.

When she cries out seconds later, victory rushes through me and I continue to lick her until her spasms start to calm. Finally, I stand, my hand ripping open my jeans and releasing my cock. Olivia's spread out before me, exactly where I want her...and I pause.

I wait for her gaze to meet mine, rein in the fierce desire to lose myself in her body because I want...no, I need something from her.

"I'd like to propose another bargain."

She's breathing heavily and it takes a few seconds for her to answer because she's watching me stroke myself. Every muscle in my body is strung tight and lust burns through my blood like lava.

"What are the terms?"

"An exclusive arrangement. You and me and this bed. I'll make you come every night you're here."

Her smile is faint but it's there. "And what do you get in return?"

"You in my bed. For as many nights as you want."

"So it's all up to me?"

"It's all your call."

Her smile widens. "Then lie down on this bed and let me have my way with you."

"I agree to your terms."

ALSO BY STEPHANIE JULIAN

SCANDALOUS DESIRE

Invite Me In

Reserve My Nights

Expose My Desire

Keep My Secrets

Rock My Heart

WICKED & CHARMING

Seducing Whitney

Claiming Ellie

Sharing Brianna

INDECENT

An Indecent Proposition

An Indecent Affair

An Indecent Arrangement

An Indecent Longing

An Indecent Desire

LOVERS UNDERCOVER

Lovers & Lies

Sinners & Secrets

Beauty & Brains

OFFSIDE HEARTS

Netting the Goalie

Pucking the Grinder

Falling for the Enforcer

Tempting the Instigator

Desiring the D-Man

Taming the Machine

Gambling on the Ghost

DEVILS HOCKEY

Rowdy Hearts

Rainbow Kisses

Rebel Secrets

Rocky's story (Title TBA)

FAST ICE

Bylines & Blue Lines

Hard Lines & Goal Lines

Deadlines & Red Lines

DARKLY ENCHANTED

Spell Bound

Moon Bound

Twice Bound

MOONLIGHT FANTASIES
Shadow Magic

Enchanted Magic

Dangerous Magic

MOONLIGHT LOVERS
Kiss of Moonlight

Visions of Moonlight

Edge of Moonlight

Temptation in Moonlight

Grace in Moonlight

Shades of Moonlight

DIVINE DESIRES
Dark Desires at Dawn

Rough Caress of Midnight

Double Fantasies at Twilight

Enchanting Temptations in Shadow

REDTAILS HOCKEY
(Third-person OFFSIDE HEARTS)

The Brick Wall

The Grinder

The Enforcer

The Instigator

The Playboy

The D-Man

The Machine

The Ghost

ABOUT THE AUTHOR

Stephanie Julian is a USA Today and New York Times best-selling author of contemporary and paranormal romance. Make sure you sign up to receive all of her news here.